"Don't lie. I know what you're up to!"

The coldness in Slade's voice sent shivers down Lisa's spine. "I don't know what you mean," she stammered.

"Don't you?" Slade taunted with arrogant challenge. "It's obvious you don't want me to handle your aunt's financial affairs. Your motive?" He smiled grimly. "So you can get your mercenary little hands on her money yourself!"

Lisa reacted with blind fury. Her palm swung in a lightning arc, striking his hard, unyielding face. Instantly Slade captured her wrist and yanked her roughly against the hard length of his body. His eyes blazed as he lowered his mouth to hers. "You aren't going to get away with that," he said savagely. "Or anything else!"

JANET DAILEY AMERICANA

LOW COUNTRY
LIAR

Harlequin Books

TORONTO • NEW YORK • LONDON
AMSTERDAM • PARIS • SYDNEY • HAMBURG
STOCKHOLM • ATHENS • TOKYO • MILAN
MADRID • WARSAW • BUDAPEST • AUCKLAND

The state flower depicted on the cover of this book is yellow jessamine.

Janet Dailey Americana edition published January 1988
Second printing October 1988
Third printing October 1989
Fourth printing October 1990
Fifth printing December 1991
Sixth printing September 1992
Seventh printing September 1992
Eighth printing September 1993

ISBN 0-373-21940-7

Harlequin Presents edition published August 1979
Second printing February 1982

Original hardcover edition published in 1978
by Mills & Boon Limited

LOW COUNTRY LIAR

CHAPTER ONE

WITH A RELAXED SIGH Lisa Talmadge leaned against the curling backrest of the chair. It was a beautifully restored antique, reupholstered in a patterned brocade of rust, orange and brown. It complemented perfectly the solid rust-colored chair her aunt sat in.

Lisa felt she had been talking nonstop since she arrived, bringing her aunt up-to-date on the latest family happenings. Soon it would be time to get down to the true reason for her visit, which was more than just a wish to see her favorite aunt. Her aunt seemed to be of the same mind.

"We've gotten rid of the preliminaries, Lisa, I now know you've had a safe trip from Baltimore. Both your parents are fine. Your brother is having girl problems as usual. You have a drink in hand to loosen your tongue, so why don't you tell me what really brought you to Charleston?"

At fifty-two, Miriam Talmadge was warm, vivacious and darkly brunette. The latter fact Lisa would never have questioned her hairdresser about. She knew that Mitzi, as Miriam Talmadge was affectionately known by those who loved her, would grow old as gracefully as she stayed young at heart.

It had been several years since Lisa had last spent any time with her aunt. Not since Mitzi had moved back to her home town of Charleston, located on the southern end of the coastal flatlands that were known to all South Carolinians as the Low Country.

Lisa didn't try to hide the smile her aunt's pointed question had prompted. "Believe it or not, Mitzi, *you* brought me to Charleston."

"Me? Goodness, that's quite a burden." A wry smile deepened the corners of her mobile mouth. "I hope you haven't sought me out about man problems. Considering the mess I made of my marriage, I'm the last one to run to for advice."

"You can't claim sole responsibility for the failure of your marriage. Uncle Simon had a part in it somewhere." Lisa dismissed the statement with a shake of her silver blond hair, a gold hooped earring glittering through the long silk strands.

"That's what Slade says, too," Mitzi Talmadge sighed.

Quickly Lisa lowered her head, her jaw tightening at the name. Her aunt had just put a name to the reason Lisa had come. For the time being, however, that was Lisa's secret until she could find out what was really going on.

"But you must remember," Mitzi was continuing, and Lisa concentrated on what she was saying, "that I was raised in an era where divorce was a scandal and a woman was supposed to make the marriage last no matter what. It's understandable, I suppose, that I should have guilt feelings regarding the failure of mine. Simon and I just weren't suited at all." There was a reflective look in her dark eyes as she smiled, her cheeks dimpling. "I married him because he was so quiet. And I divorced him because he was *so* quiet," she laughed. "Which proves what an eternal romantic I am at heart, doesn't it? I was all caught up in the image of the strong, silent type when that wasn't what I really wanted or needed. Poor Simon didn't get any bargain with me either. I was so disorganized when it came to anything outside of my writing that it drove him to distraction. He wanted the unobtrusive, home-making kind of wife who always had a delicious meal ready at promptly seven o'clock. I could barely boil water without a crisis. Ours was a very sad mismatch, but I'm glad he had a few happy years with his second wife before he died," she concluded.

"What about you, Mitzi? You've had time to meet somebody new?" The question was put innocently, but there was a sharp edge to the look in Lisa's olive green eyes. "Tell me about the men in your life."

"Men in the plural? You make me sound like a femme fatale. At my age!" Mitzi shook her head laughingly, a bright twinkle in her eyes. "You're going to be awfully good for my morale, Lisa. And exactly how did the subject get around to my love life when I asked about yours?"

"I thought I'd dodged the question rather expertly." Lisa smiled broadly. "The fact is at the present time I don't have a love life."

"I find that extremely hard to believe. You've grown into a beautiful woman, Lisa Talmadge, with your mother's cheekbones and her blond hair. Those green eyes are definitely from the Talmadge side, outlined with sooty lashes just the way Simon's were. They're definitely your most striking feature. But you're side-tracking me again," Mitzi scolded with mock reproof.

"Now why have you come? Did you break up with some special man?"

"No. There isn't anyone 'special.'" Lisa raised her hands, making mock quotation marks with her fingers. "I'm escaping from nothing but work," she insisted.

"And that young man you were engaged to?" Mitzi prompted, tipping her head slightly downward to watch Lisa's expression closely.

"Michel? That was over three years ago when I graduated from college." Lisa picked up her cocktail, touching a forefinger to the lime wedge floating on top and watching it bob in the liquid.

"What really happened between you two?"

"A conflict of careers. He wanted a country-club wife and I wanted to work—that's why I'd got my degree. He didn't see it that way. To him, my education was supposed to be just a safeguard for my future in case anything ever happened to him. In the meantime he wanted me home taking care of him and raising a family." Lisa shrugged. The bitterness had long since fled. "I didn't object to that as much as I objected to him telling me that was what I wanted. It's just as well, because it would never have worked between us."

"You're not sorry, then?" Mitzi prompted.

"Not a bit," Lisa returned without any regret. "Now I just steer clear of the strong, masterful types like Michel with their super male egos that constantly have to be fed."

"You said you were escaping from your job. Hasn't it turned out to be what you wanted?" The older woman relaxed in the cushioned chair, its rusty orange a pleasant contrast to her dark coloring. "Your last letter seemed filled with complaints about staff and management."

"I think you can mark that up to almost a year and a half without a vacation rather than the job," Lisa stated, following her aunt's suit and leaning back in her chair. "Since the television station gave the go-ahead on the new show a year ago, it's been hectic, to say the least, but very rewarding and satisfying. I'd only worked as an assistant on other shows. This is the first one I've produced myself, so I put in a lot of hours to prove myself, postponing my vacation, certain the show would fall apart without me. Finally I realized I would fall apart if I didn't get away for a while."

"So you came here." Mitzi's curiosity over Lisa's choice was still evident.

"I couldn't think of a better place than Charleston. Time seems to pass so leisurely here. Plus, I have you for company," Lisa concluded, keeping to herself the other very pertinent reason for her choice.

"For whatever reason, I'm glad you're here for a few weeks. I only hope you don't find it too boring after the exciting life you've been leading working in television." Before Lisa had a chance to refute her aunt's statement, Mitzi Talmadge made one of her lightning changes of subject. One thought often triggered off another in Mitzi's mind; it was a trait that was characteristic of her personality. "Do you remember the letter you wrote me when you first went to work for the broadcasting company? I can't help laughing when I think about it. You'd put in your application and were so irate when they called you back to hire you as their weather girl."

"At the time, I was a very militant feminist," Lisa

agreed with a laughing smile. "I hope I've mellowed with age."

"Mellowed with age—and you're all of twenty-four," her aunt mocked.

"You don't know how vocal a Women's Libber I was," Lisa declared. "When I think of the lecture I gave the company about their weather-girl job, I wonder why they ever hired me!"

"That's what Slade said. I told him about the incident when I heard you were coming for a visit."

The mention of his name set Lisa's teeth on edge. She attempted a bright smile. "I'm dying to meet this paragon you call Slade Blackwell. You've mentioned him half a dozen times in your letters." A half a hundred would have been closer.

"I would have invited him to dinner this evening, but because it's your first night here, I thought it would be best with just the two of us. I promise you that you'll meet him soon. Maybe tomorrow night," suggested Mitzi Talmadge as the idea began to form in her mind.

"I believe you said he was the son of an old family friend?" Lisa's tongue felt almost honey coated as she made the casual inquiry—too sweet to be sincere—but Mitzi didn't seem to notice.

"Mmm, yes," Mitzi sipped her drink, replying absently. "I met him quite by accident shortly after I moved back here to Charleston when my divorce from Simon was final. If you remember, my mother died soon after my divorce, so I really had a very trying few months."

"I can imagine," Lisa murmured.

"But Slade was wonderful," Mitzi continued, not

hearing Lisa's low comment. "I never had a head for business—not that I'm as stupid as some people, but I just find it very tedious and dull. Anyway, things became quite complicated with the divorce and the settlement of the family estate. Slade simply took over for me and handled everything. You know how I loathe details, Lisa," Mitzi smiled at herself. "Now that Slade is looking after everything I don't have to be bothered with them. He makes out all the checks and all I have to do is sign them."

With sinking heart, Lisa felt as if her worst suspicions had been confirmed. How could her aunt be so gullible? Her letters this past year had been filled with "Slade said," "Slade suggested," or "Slade told me." He had been quoted as a veritable authority on anything and everything.

It was at Slade Blackwell's instigation that Mitzi had reopened the family home in Old Charleston. Lisa remembered that it also had been the interior decorator he had recommended who had been given the task of renovating the mansion.

Her green gaze swept the living room with its high ceilings and rich cypress woodwork. Lisa was unable to find fault with the completed product. The decor was a smooth mix of antique and modern. It invited a guest to sit back and relax, instead of giving a museum effect that said, Fragile, Keep Off.

Yet it grated, just as it grated to know that Slade Blackwell had suggested the landscape architect for the walled garden outside the colonnade portico. In the waning hours of a March dusk, it was ablaze with spring flowers—azaleas and camellias and the magnolia trees budding, the scent of honeysuckle drifting in the air. Magnificent spreading oaks dominated it all with their elegant draping of silvery beardlike moss.

The same company that designed the garden still maintained it. Lisa couldn't help wondering what kind of a kickback Slade Blackwell made out of the deal. Those two items were just the obvious ones; she guessed there were many other small deals as well. Now Mitzi had informed her that Slade Blackwell made out the checks for her signature. Lisa doubted if Mitzi even verified what she was signing. The man was probably stealing her blind.

"Does this Mr. Blackwell handle all your money?" There was a faint challenge in Lisa's question. She simply couldn't keep it out even though she tried.

"All except some that I keep in an account of my own. I call it my mad money." An impish smile made the woman appear even younger.

Heaven only knew how much was in that account! Heaven or Slade Blackwell—Lisa wouldn't even hazard a guess. She did know that her aunt had received a considerable amount from Simon Talmadge when they had divorced. Lisa's father had understood that Mitzi's mother had been quite wealthy and Mitzi had been an only child.

Plus, there was the income Mitzi made writing romance mysteries. The latter wasn't a large sum, but combined with the other, it was probably a sizeable amount that Mitzi Talmadge was worth.

"Aren't you worried that you're a bit too trusting, Mitzi?" Lisa set her glass on the ornate coaster sitting atop a marble inlaid table, trying to disguise the sharpness of her tone.

"Do you mean where Slade is concerned?" There was faint surprise in the woman's answering question. Then she laughed, a gay melodious sound. "A more honest, dependable man couldn't be found. You haven't met him yet, but when you do, I know you'll like him." Mitzi hesitated, her gaze sharpening. "On second thought, maybe you won't."

"Oh?" Lisa was instantly alert. "Why?"

"You said a moment ago that you have an aversion for the strong, masterful type. I'm afraid those adjectives would fit Slade. Of course, he can be very charming and gracious, too."

When it suits him to be. Lisa added the qualification silently. An older woman probably seemed an easy target to Slade Blackwell. Mitzi didn't have any close family—her parents dead, no aunts or uncles living, the husband she had divorced gone, too. What money he didn't steal from her while she was alive he probably hoped to inherit on her death.

"What did he say when he learned I was coming for a visit?" Lisa asked.

"I don't recall that Slade said anything in particular except that he was glad Simon's family hadn't forgotten me."

"We didn't forget you," Lisa protested quickly. Anger against this Slade Blackwell slowly began to grow hotter. No doubt he wanted Mitzi to be isolated and totally dependent on him.

"I didn't mean to imply that you had," her aunt hastened with a dismissing laugh. "But you must admit it was awkward when Simon was alive. After all, he was your father's brother and we were divorced. I couldn't very well be included as if nothing had changed. I wouldn't have wanted it that way if your parents had tried."

"Well, as far as I'm concerned, you are still part of my family," Lisa stated emphatically, "regardless of any divorce."

"God love you, Lisa," Mitzi laughed. "I still think of you as my niece, too. That's why I'm so glad you've come for a visit." Just as quickly, she became thoughtful. "There's only one thing I regret in my life. Oh, not the years I spent with Simon," she assured Lisa hastily. "But the fact that we never had any children and that Simon wouldn't adopt any. You seem like my own daughter, though, and Slade my son."

"Is Slade Blackwell related to you?" Lisa questioned. It suddenly occurred to her that he might be some distant relation.

"No," Mitzi denied somewhat ruefully. "His father once proposed to me, though, many years ago. Sometimes, when I'm in a really sentimental mood, I start thinking that if I'd married him instead of Simon, Slade would be my son. But of course, I didn't and he isn't and it's all water under the bridge." She dismissed the subject with a wave of her hand and a smile. "Tell me what you would like to do while you're in Charleston."

"Don't worry about entertaining me." Lisa folded her hands in her lap, relaxing more fully into the cushioned chair. "I know you're in the middle of a book. You just keep right on writing and I'll wander around on my own. I have a couple of people I want to look up while I'm here."

"College friends?"

"More or less," she answered without lying.

But her true plans were just beginning to take shape. One of the very first things she was going to do was meet this Slade Blackwell and find out what his game was. She was determined to accomplish her plan without her aunt present.

If there was one thing she had learned producing the local affairs show, it was how to handle people. And more importantly, how to ask the questions that would reveal a person's true stand, either by doing it herself, or having a reporter do it for her. Slade Blackwell was going to have quite a few questions to answer.

Mitzi glanced at her wristwatch. "Goodness, it's past seven!" She frowned and looked toward the dining room with its small teardrop chandelier suspended above a gleaming white-clothed table. "Mildred usually serves promptly at seven. I wonder what's wrong."

As if on cue, the housekeeper-cook and general dogsbody appeared. There was an exasperated thinness to the line of her mouth, a grimness to her features that said she had put up with more than her share of troubles.

"As near as I can tell, dinner is going to be about thirty minutes late tonight. The oven is on the blink again," she announced, her tone saying it was just about the last straw.

"Oh, no!" Mitzi echoed the housekeeper's sentiment, plus an additional note that indicated she didn't want to be bothered with the problem. "Didn't Slade say that he knew—".

"I've already phoned Slade," the housekeeper

replied, using his given name calmly. "He'll have the man out first thing in the morning. But in the meantime, dinner will be late."

Lisa waited until the housekeeper returned to the kitchen before asking, "Couldn't you have called your own repairman, Mitzi?"

"I suppose so," was the answer, as though it hadn't occurred to her before Lisa suggested it. "But it's so much easier to call Slade. He always knows a reliable firm to send."

Yes, Lisa thought cynically, one that will be certain to reward him for passing on business. And a house as old as this was costly to maintain. Several trades would be involved. It seemed to Lisa that what had begun as merely a suspicion against Slade Blackwell was proving to be a well-founded one.

"It isn't that difficult to find a reliable company," Lisa insisted. "It would require a few phone calls and some checking, but you could do it and not have to rely on someone else."

"Oh, I could do anything if I set my mind to it," Mitzi agreed with an expansive wave of her hand. "The trouble is that I am so lazy."

"I find that hard to believe. Look at your writing schedule," she argued.

"Ah, but that is something that I enjoy doing. It isn't work. As far as anything else goes, I don't want to be bothered," she said with an uncaring shrug. "If I didn't have Slade to turn to, I probably would take care of these routine matters. But I do have him. He spoils me outrageously and I love it."

What could she say to that, Lisa wondered. Her

aunt was an intelligent woman. Why couldn't she make her see that she was vulnerable? Or, perhaps the word was gullible?

Dinner was eventually served about a quarter of an hour later than Mildred had thought. The evening passed quite pleasantly despite the prolonged serving time. The conversation was filled with reminiscences of old times and gossip about family. The only irritant Lisa found was the way Slade Blackwell's name kept cropping up.

Mildred plodded into the living room to the low, marble-inlaid table in front of the sofa. She picked up the empty coffee service as if it weighed a ton and started to leave. At Mitzi's chair, she paused.

"Will you be wanting anything else tonight, Mitzi?" But she didn't give her employer an opportunity to answer. "If you don't, I'll be turning in now." Her heavily intoned words implied that she was on her last legs, and any further requests would be a severe strain on her health.

"I am sure there is nothing else we will need," Lisa's aunt responded with a sympathetic smile. "Have a good night, Mildred."

"I'll try," was the sighing reply as the housekeeper shuffled out of the room. She made it appear that it was too much of an effort to pick up her feet.

When the housekeeper was out of sight, Mitzi's twinkling gaze slid to Lisa. "Isn't she a character? She could do the work of an army, but she gives the impression that the smallest task is too much for her. Bless her grumbling soul. I don't know what I'd do without her. Slade found her, of course."

"Of course," Lisa echoed dryly and tried to swallow a yawn, but she couldn't.

"You're tired, aren't you? I had forgotten how exhausting it is to travel. I'll bet you'd like to have an early night."

"Oh, no, really," Lisa started to protest.

"Don't argue. You are tired. We'll have plenty of time to talk in the next two weeks. There isn't any need to try to do all our talking in one night," Mitzi insisted.

Lisa *was* tired and didn't object at all to having her arm twisted. "If you are sure you don't mind...."

"I don't mind. Do you remember which room you have?" Her aunt rose and Lisa did likewise.

"Yes, I remember. Turn right at the top of the stairs and it's the second room," she recalled.

"That's it. I'll be turning in now, too. I'll be rising with the sun to work on my novel, but you sleep as late as you wish," her aunt instructed. "Remember, you're on vacation."

"Which means not dashing about to get to work," Lisa smiled. She started toward the foyer and the staircase leading to the second floor. Over her shoulder, she added, "And thanks for letting me spend my vacation here."

"Thanks aren't necessary. I am proud to have you here. Good night."

"Good night, Mitzi," Lisa waved as she rounded the opened double doors into the foyer.

The staircase of heavily carved and polished cypress made a lazy circle to the second floor. Lisa climbed its carpeted steps, a hand sliding along the smooth wood of the carved banister to the top. The plaster walls of the upper-floor hallway were painted a pearl white. The color gave light to the high-ceilinged but narrow corridor.

Turning right, Lisa entered the second room. Her previous inspection of the room had been a cursory one, a hurried tour on her arrival, cut short by her desire to return downstairs to visit with her aunt. Now she let her gaze wander around the room.

Mitzi had said she had specifically chosen that guest room for Lisa because it seemed to be "her." The walls were a rich jade green, accented by woodwork painted ivory. A small alcove held a sofa decorated in vivid greens and golds. The silklike material of the drapes was of ivory to match the bedspread on the canopied bed. The area rug was patterned in an Oriental design that incorporated the green and off-white colors with a vivid yellow.

The sight of her suitcases standing at the foot of the bed reminded Lisa that she hadn't yet unpacked. She sighed tiredly, then noticed her nightgown and robe lying across the bed. She picked up one suitcase. It was light as a feather. Setting it back down, Lisa walked to the closet. All her clothes were there, neatly hung on wire hangers. The rest of her things were in the drawers of a Provençal-styled dresser. The housekeeper had obviously unpacked the suitcases for her.

"Bless her grumbling soul." Lisa repeated her aunt's earlier comment about Mildred, murmuring it in all sincerity.

Kicking off her shoes, she walked to a second ivory-painted door. It opened into a private bathroom where her cosmetics were arranged neatly on the counter in front of a well-lighted vanity mirror. There wasn't anything left for her to do.

Lisa glanced at the large porcelain bathtub with its gold fixtures and green and gold shower curtain, but the bed looked infinitely more inviting at the moment. Closing the bathroom door, she changed into her nightclothes.

Climbing between the clean-scented sheets of the bed, she switched off the light on the stand beside the bed. Lisa stared at the pale silk of the canopy above her head. Tomorrow she would be meeting Slade Blackwell. She wanted to be very well rested for that. She closed her eyes.

As Lisa followed the descending rail of the spiral staircase the next morning, she could hear the staccato tapping of typewriter keys coming from the downstairs study. Smiling to herself, she knew she wouldn't have to make any explanations to Mitzi. Her aunt was hard at work on her new novel.

At the bottom of the stairs, Lisa paused in front of the large oval mirror to make a last-minute inspection of her appearance. The loose-fitting waistcoat-type jacket gave height to her average build, the skirt long enough to be fashionable while revealing the shapely curve of her legs. The waistcoat and skirt were spring green in color over a complementing brightly printed blouse with long sleeves.

Hats had become her passion in the last year and Lisa wore one now, a matching green turban that gave a touch of sophistication to the overall effect. A silkily blond wisp of hair had escaped the hat, trailing the curve of her neck. Lisa tucked it beneath the hat and adjusted the large gold stud of her earring.

Satisfaction sparkled in her eyes, their color enhanced by the green of her outfit. She liked the image of the woman looking back at her, professional yet definitely feminine. Her gaze slid to the bone-colored handbag in her left hand. Inside was a slip of paper with Slade Blackwell's business address.

Lisa had no doubt he would see her this morning, regardless of whether or not she had an appointment. He wouldn't turn away the niece of Mitzi Talmadge. Once she was inside the door, he would not find it so easy to be rid of her.

"Would you like breakfast now, miss?"

Glancing toward the sound of the voice, Lisa saw the long-suffering Mildred standing just inside the doorway and smiled. "No, thank you, Mildred. I function much better on an empty stomach."

"Beg pardon?"

"It doesn't matter." Lisa didn't bother with an explanation of her statement and ran a smoothing hand over her hip. "If Mitzi asks where I am, tell her I've gone to see an old friend."

As often as she had heard Blackwell's name in the past twenty-four hours, it did feel as if she had known him a long time and disliked him for an equal length.

"Will you be home for lunch, then?" Mildred inquired in a voice that was wearily patient.

Lisa hesitated. "No," she decided. "I'll be back sometime in the afternoon. What time is Mitzi generally through for the day?"

"It depends, miss. It depends," was the answer, indicating that anything more definite was quite beyond her.

Concealing the amused smile that tugged at the

corners of her mouth, Lisa wished the housekeeper a good day and walked out of the ornately carved front door into the midmorning of a March day. The air was balmy, the sun bright, not a hint of a blustery March wind to be found.

The lovely old mansion was narrow and long. The house didn't actually front the narrow street in Old Charleston; its entrance door opened onto the portico running the length of one side. Lisa's heels clicked noisily on the smooth stone as she walked to the false house door opening onto the street from the portico. Closing it behind her, she heard the rumble of carriage wheels and the steady clop of horses' hooves. Lisa paused to watch a horse-drawn surrey around the narrow street corner, its fringe waving with the motion.

Tourists sat in the seats behind the guide, taking a carriage tour of Old Charleston. They had obviously seen her coming from the mansion, Lisa realized, and they stared openly. She smiled and waved, knowing they believed she was a full-fledged Charlestonian instead of a tourist like themselves.

The carriage ride looked like a fun way to tour Old Charleston, whose history encompassed the Southern manner of gracious living, the sad days of the Civil War, and beyond that, the era of Colonial America. Lisa glanced around the immediate neighborhood. Magnolia trees and massive oaks, with their leaves and branches draped by Spanish moss, towered beside and above fine old homes. The colorful splash of flowers seemed to be in every lawn and garden, creeping along fences and spouting from stone urns.

Lisa squared her shoulders. There would be time enough to do some sight-seeing later on. For the time being; she couldn't be distracted by the beauty around her, not until after she'd had her confrontation with Slade Blackwell. The click of her heels made a purposeful sound as she started out.

It was a short walk along the stagecoach-wide street to Meeting Street, where Lisa was able to obtain directions to the law offices of Courtney Blackwell & Son. Slade Blackwell was, of course, the "Son." The office, too, was located in Old Charleston, in an old merchant building with ornate cornice trim around the roof.

The instant Lisa entered the offices she had the impression of a small, exclusive practice. Richly paneled walls, their wood gleaming with the patina of years, emitted a studious air, while antiques and plush leather furniture added intimacy to the overall atmosphere.

The receptionist was an older woman with sleekly coiffed gray hair. She wore glasses with half lenses which she peered over at Lisa. Yet she managed to exude an attitude of polite deference.

"May I help you?"

"I'm here to see Mr. Slade Blackwell." Lisa didn't bother to inform the woman she didn't have an appointment nor that he didn't know her.

Surprisingly no questions were put to her as the woman nodded her head toward a set of carved oak double doors. "His office is through those doors."

This was going to be easier than she had thought. No preliminary introductions to be forwarded to him. No explanations as to why she was there. Slade Blackwell was proving to be much more accessible than she had believed.

The doors opened to a small office, complete with desk, typewriter and filing cabinets. Obviously it was supposed to be manned by his private secretary, but there was no one in sight to greet Lisa. Closing the doors, she walked into the office, deciding it had been partitioned from a larger room.

An overstuffed leather armchair was in a corner with an old wooden magazine rack and smokestand beside it, but Lisa didn't take its invitation to sit and wait. Instead she walked to the vacant secretary's desk. Except for an opened appointment book, it was tidily swept clean of any papers.

She glanced cautiously toward the door leading to Slade Blackwell's private office. There were no sounds coming from it, but the walls of the building were thick. Carefully she slid the appointment book around to peep at his day's agenda.

Without warning the door was opened, and Lisa nearly jumped out of her shoes. She quickly concealed her start of guilty surprise to inspect the man confronting her. His tall, leanly muscled build was clothed in an impeccably tailored suit of oyster gray, complete with waistcoat.

There the lawyer image ended and the man began. And he made an immediate physical impact on Lisa. The breath she had been holding she released slowly, then seemed unable to take another. Every nerve in her body quivered with the alertness of an animal scenting danger.

This was Slade Blackwell. Lisa needed no introduction. If she had expected the suave image of a Southern gentleman, chivalrous and courtly, charming a rich widow with his pearly smile, she would have needed to make an immediate reassessment. Somehow, though, Lisa hadn't got as far as picturing her opponent.

Strong and masterful, Mitzi had described him. Meek words, Lisa concluded silently. Belligerently male, he was as hard as a piece of granite that had somehow managed to come to life. He exuded an air of vitality that seemed to smother, a sensual power that was overwhelming. At least, Lisa felt its suffocating force.

Raven-black hair grew thickly away from his forehead, seeming to appear waywardly casual in its style. His eyes were the color of his hair, burning like black coals yet possessing the sharpness of an eagle. No gentle spaniel-brown eyes for Slade Blackwell.

Tanned lean cheeks, faintly hollowed, accented the angular slant of his jaw to a thrusting chin. There was an unyielding firmness to his mouth that seemed to suggest a latent ruthlessness in getting what he wanted. Dark, thick brows managed to appear finely drawn. One was arched slightly higher than the other now in arrogant censure.

"It's about time you arrived." His voice was low pitched. It might have been pleasant had his tone not been sharpened by tightly leashed impatience. "The agency had assured me they would have someone here by nine-thirty. It is now half past ten. There are some important letters that need to be out right away. They're on the dictaphone. I presume you do know how to operate a dictaphone?"

On the last dryly sarcastic note, he pivoted on his heel and reentered his private office.

CHAPTER TWO

THE SHARP CLICK of the closing door snapped Lisa out of her daze. Her mouth opened. The words formed to call him back, her hand raised uselessly. Then she hesitated, her hand coming back to her mouth as she began to thoughtfully nibble a fingernail.

Why not? a mischievous little voice inside her demanded.

Obviously Slade Blackwell was expecting a replacement for his regular secretary and had mistaken Lisa for that replacement. Why should she bother to tell him differently? A private secretary would have access to all the files. If she wanted proof to confirm or denounce her suspicions, what better way than through his own records?

It was a heaven-sent opportunity. She would be a fool not to take advantage of it. True, Lisa admitted, she wasn't trained as a secretary, but she could type, not very speedily, but at least it wasn't the hunt-and-peck method. She knew the rudiments of dictaphone use. With any luck she could bluff her way through what other skills might be necessary.

With the decision made, Lisa quickly stepped behind the desk, slipping her bag into a lower drawer. The first thing she had to do was cancel the order for a secretary. She had no idea which agency had been contacted and couldn't very well ask. That meant going down the list of agencies in the telephone book and calling every one until she found the right one. Luckily, she reached the right agency on the third call.

One more phone call. She looked the number up in the directory and dialed it quickly. Her fingers drummed the desktop impatiently as she listened to the ring on the other end.

Finally it was answered. "Talmadge residence," came the world-weary voice of the housekeeper.

"Mildred, this is Lisa." She hurried her words, speaking softly and quickly. "I'm just calling to let you know my... my friends and I are going to make an afternoon of it. Tell Mitzi I'll be back shortly after five o'clock."

"Did she tell you?"

Lisa frowned at the receiver. "Tell me what?"

"That Sl—Mr. Blackwell is coming for dinner tonight." The housekeeper immediately corrected herself to refer to their guest formally.

"Good lord," Lisa muttered to herself, seeing all sorts of complications setting in. "What time is he to be there?"

"He usually comes for cocktails around six," was the reply.

"I'll be there by then." An irritated "damn" slipped out as Lisa replaced the receiver on the hook.

But there wasn't time to dwell on her ultimate unmasking. She had to start transcribing the letters on the dictaphone before Slade Blackwell became suspicious about the silence in his outer office. It took a few minutes to find the stationery and carbon paper, and another few minutes to figure out how to operate the dictaphone before she was finally able to start.

On the first letter, the spacing and margins were all wrong. The result was decidedly amateurish and Lisa had to do it all over again, interrupted by phone calls that she had to transfer to Slade Blackwell. The metal cabinets kept beckoning Lisa to investigate their files, but she remembered his statement that the letters were important. She didn't want Slade Blackwell coming out to discover her going through the files when she should be typing.

Working on the fourth—and what she hoped was the last—letter, Lisa heard the connecting office door open and mentally tensed as Slade Blackwell stopped at her desk. Her cool green eyes slid a brief glance in his direction as he picked up the letters she had finished. She tried to increase her typing speed to an efficient rate—a mistake, as she misspelled a word by reversing the letters. She reached quickly for the liquid paper to correct it.

The longest letter of those she had completed was tossed back to her desk. "The word is 'guaranty,' not 'guarantee,' Miss—?"

"Mrs. Eldridge." The false name came so quickly to her tongue that Lisa was slightly astounded. Quickly she used her little finger to turn the birthstone ring on her left finger around so a plain gold band showed. "Mrs. Ann Eldridge," she carried her lie further, using her middle name in place of her first.

"The word is repeated several times in the letter, Mrs. Eldridge. You'll have to retype it," he declared with cutting indifference.

"Of course," Lisa agreed with a nod of deference, but she was actually gritting her teeth. He seemed to be waiting for an explanation for her error, and Lisa grudgingly gave him one, masking it in sweet politeness. "Unfortunately I'm not familiar with the 'to wits and 'whereas' and the other legal terminology, Mr. Blackwell."

"I specifically requested a legal secretary," he stated.

"The agency didn't have anyone available with legal experience. I'm sorry."

She didn't dare look at him as she made the false apology. Lisa knew the glint in her eye was anything but apologetic. She could feel his sharp gaze studying her and tried to ignore the uncomfortable sensation it aroused.

"Do you always wear a hat when you work, Mrs. Eldridge?"

Her hand lifted to her head in surprise, her fingers touching the green turban covering her silver blond hair. She hadn't completely forgotten about it, and a germ of an idea immediately took hold.

"Only when my hair is a mess, Mr. Blackwell." This time she met his arrogantly appraising look, smiling faintly with a touch of challenge.

One corner of his mouth quirked as if he found some cynical form of amusement in her answer, but he made no further comment about the hat.

"I have a luncheon appointment. I'll be back around one o'clock," he told her, and walked to the double doors leading to the reception area.

Waiting, Lisa listened for the opening and closing of the outside door before she darted from the desk to the metal filing cabinets. Alone at last, she had her first chance to investigate the files. She tried not to think about how unethical her search was, if not downright dishonest.

Filing systems were beyond her experience, but luckily the drawers seemed to be labeled. Quickly Lisa began looking for the one that might indicate that it contained her aunt's records. The door to the reception area opened and Lisa stared visibly again.

"Hello." A man walked in, shorter than Slade Blackwell but in his age group of the late thirties. He wore glasses and his brown hair was combed forward across his forehead; Lisa suspected it was to conceal a receding hairline. "You must be Mary Lou's replacement."

"Yes, I am." Lisa heard the nervous tremor in her voice and tried to return the man's broad smile naturally. She glanced toward the connecting door to Slade Blackwell's office. "I'm sorry, but Mr. Blackwell has just left for lunch."

"Yes, I know. I saw him in the reception area before he left," was the answer, but the man made no move to leave.

Her fingers were resting on the handle of one drawer. The metal felt almost hot to the touch. It was so obvious that she was looking for something that she couldn't move away from the cabinets. She silently cursed the inner sensation of guilt that made her so uncomfortable.

"Was there something I could help you with?" she asked politely, wishing he would go.

The man was staring at her, his expression making it plain that he liked what he saw. Her prodding question seemed to awaken him from his silent study.

"Yes," he walked quickly towards her. "I came to get the Talmadge file."

"The what?" Lisa breathed weakly.

"Talmadge, Miriam L.," he repeated, not apparently noticing the way the color drained from her face.

She turned away from him, mentally grasping for straws. "I'm sorry, but these are Mr. Blackwell's files. I couldn't possibly—"

"Good heavens!" he interrupted with a laugh. "I didn't introduce myself, did I? I'm Slade's assistant, consultant or whatever label you want to pin on me." He extended a hand to Lisa. "The name is Drew, as in Andrew, Rutledge—unfortunately no relation to the Charlestonian Rutledges of yore. And you are?"

"L—" Inadvertently she almost gave him her real name and caught herself just in time. "Ann Eldridge. Mrs. Ann Eldridge."

When Lisa had first placed her hand in his, he had seemed inclined to hold it. He released it on hearing her marital status, a faintly rueful smile curving his mouth.

"Divorced? Widowed?" Drew Rutledge inquired with mock hopefulness.

Lisa had to add another lie to the rest. "As of this morning when I left the house and kissed my husband goodbye, I was neither of those."

"Isn't that just my luck?" he grinned. "The first attractive secretary we get in this place turns out to be married. Happily, I suppose?"

"Very happily married," Lisa lied again.

"Pity," Drew sighed mockingly, and shook his head. "I guess I'll have to retreat to the ranks of the confirmed bachelors with Slade."

"Mr. Blackwell isn't married?" Somehow she had never assumed that he was. Now it was confirmed.

"No. We've had a standing bet since our college days as to which of us gets married first, and we've both had our share of close calls."

"Haven't we all?" Lisa agreed dryly, thinking of her abortive engagement to Michel, but her remark drew a curious look from Drew. She had to cover the slip quickly. "But once you meet the right person you don't want to settle for a close call."

"So I've heard," he smiled, the curiosity leaving his hazel eyes at her reply. "Well, I suppose I'd better let you get back to work."

"Yes." She tried not to show her relief. "I have a lot to do."

"I'll get out of your way and let you get at it, as soon as you hand me the Talmadge file," he agreed.

Her hope that Drew had forgotten the reason he had come in faded with his statement. She hesitated. "I really don't think I should—"

"You guard the files more jealously than Mary Lou does," he laughed.

Lisa seized on that comment instantly. "If that's true, then that's all the more reason for me not to give it to you." The main reason, of course, was that she wanted to look at it herself. "If it's not common practice to let the files leave this office, I shouldn't give it to you."

"I have work to do, too, but I can't do it without the file," he insisted patiently, amused by her reluctance.

"Listen, I'm just a temporary," Lisa pointed out. "Maybe you should wait until after lunch when Mr.

Blackwell comes back." That would give her an opportunity to look at the file's contents before she handed it over to him.

"He's the one who sent me in here to get it," Drew replied. "He would have mentioned it to you, I'm sure, if he'd known you were going to turn into a green dragon guarding the file cabinets." His gaze flicked briefly and mockingly to the green suit she was wearing.

There weren't any more excuses left. She had used them all. Inwardly she railed against the fates that had brought him in here for the Talmadge file and no other. Here she was with the ideal chance to do some undercover work and the object of her inquiry was being removed.

"I promise I won't let the file out of my sight and return it the minute I'm through." Drew raised two fingers. "Scout's honor."

"All right," Lisa agreed very grudgingly. She looked at the metal cabinets and found herself back in the same dilemma. Which drawer was it in? "Do you know where it's filed? I don't know this system." Or any system, other than the helter-skelter one in her own office in Baltimore.

"I'll find it," Drew offered, and Lisa stepped aside. He opened the very drawer her hand had been resting on and flipped through the alphabetical index to the T's. "Here it is."

Lisa had a fleeting glimpse of her aunt's name on the tab before he tucked it under his arm and closed the drawer. It was frustrating to know how close she had been to it and to see it being taken away.

"Don't look so upset," Drew teased. "I'll have it back first thing tomorrow. I hope," he tacked on as a qualifying afterthought.

"I'm not upset. Not really." Lisa composed herself quickly. "I was just wondering if anyone else would be coming in asking for files." She latched on to the first excuse that came to mind.

"No need to worry," he assured her. "There's only myself, Slade and Ellen Tyler at the reception desk. Bob Tucker, the other assistant, consultant, whatever to Slade, isn't here. He should be back this weekend, although Mary Lou took a two-week leave of absence."

"Mary Lou? Mr. Blackwell's secretary, the one I'm replacing?"

"She's also Bob's wife. There was a death in her family," Drew explained. "After two weeks here, you'll know your way around the office and filing system like a pro."

"I may not be here for two weeks." *Not when Slade Blackwell discovers who I really am*, Lisa thought.

"Why not?" He cocked his head curiously, his eyebrows puckering together.

"I'm not a trained legal secretary. The agency didn't have one available when Mr. Blackwell called. They'll be replacing me with someone more experienced."

Her gaze kept darting to the file under his arm. Lisa turned away to walk back to her desk before Drew noticed her preoccupation with the folder.

"I'll put in a word with Slade to keep you on until Mary Lou comes back. Experience doesn't count for all that much in this place. Slade likes things done his way, which is not necessarily according to the book."

I can believe that, Lisa thought cynically, but she kept her opinion to herself.

"That's kind of you," she said aloud instead, "but Mr. Blackwell might have his own opinion."

"I know what he'll say." Drew nodded positively. "He'll tell me the same thing his father always tells me—that I'm a sucker for a pretty face."

"His father? The Courtney Blackwell of Courtney Blackwell & Son?"

"That's right, the old man himself."

"Has he retired?" Lisa asked. "You didn't mention him when you ran down the list of people in the office."

"He retired within a year after Slade got his law degree." Drew walked to Lisa's desk, leaning against the edge, hooking a knee over the corner so he was half sitting on the top. "He didn't like practicing law, said he was a farmer at heart, but there's been a Blackwell practicing law in Charleston for years. When Slade qualified, the tradition was carried on through him and Court moved out to the country."

"He's farming, then."

"Yes, he bought what was the old Blackwell plantation that the family had lost after the Civil War. The original house was still standing, but one wing was beyond repair and had to be torn down. They've restored most of it, though. It's quite a place," he smiled. "You should see it."

"Sounds interesting." But Lisa was wondering if Slade Blackwell was contributing Mitzi's money to the restoration.

"Is your husband the jealous type?" Drew asked unexpectedly.

"Burt?" Lisa was stunned. She couldn't believe the

way these lies and fake names were springing from her tongue. She just hoped she could keep them all straight. "No, he's not particularly jealous. Why?"

"I'd like to take you to lunch tomorrow. I'd make it for today, but I have this—" he touched the folder under his arm, "—to work on. Which means I'll have to settle for Ellen bringing me back a sandwich." He noticed her hesitation and teased, "Come on, Ann. I'm harmless. Just look at me—I wear glasses, I'm short, or at least shorter than Slade. But I have a great personality. Perfectly harmless, I promise."

"I'll bet you are," she laughed with mocking skepticism.

"What do you say? Is it a date?" Drew wasn't put off.

"Ask me tomorrow." *If I'm here,* Lisa added to herself.

"I'll do that." He started to straighten from the desk, glancing at the watch on his wrist. "Talking about lunch, if you want yours today, you'd better be leaving. Things get pretty hectic around here in the afternoons."

Lisa looked at her own watch, realizing how swiftly the time had fled since Slade Blackwell had left. It was nearly noon and her stomach was beginning to protest its hunger after skipping breakfast that morning. Mentally she thumbed her nose at the unfinished letter in the typewriter carriage and opened the lower desk drawer where she had put her purse.

"That's a good idea," she told Drew. "I think I will leave now."

Later, sitting alone in a booth at a nearby small restaurant crowded with lunch-hour patrons, Lisa stared at the few crumbs left that had been her lunch. She had had time to think while she was eating and she was just beginning to recognize what a very complicated and potentially embarrassing situation she had got into with her lies.

Drew Rutledge had the folder Lisa wanted to read and he wouldn't return it before tomorrow. Which was too late. That left her with two choices. The first was to go back to the office and tell Slade Blackwell who she really was before he discovered it for himself.

But how could she possibly explain why she hadn't done it before? Lisa didn't think he had all that great a sense of humor to laugh off her masquerade.

The second alternative was to continue the deception until she could get her hands on the records concerning her aunt and take the risk of being unmasked before she could succeed. The only way she could do that was by avoiding meeting Slade Blackwell as herself, Lisa Talmadge.

Considering her aunt had invited him to dinner this evening, that was already impossible. He would recognize her instantly. Then she would have to be the one who did all the explaining instead of the other way around.

Sighing, Lisa glanced out the restaurant window. The sunlight hit the glass at just the right angle to reflect her own image. Her green eyes focused on the blurred reflection of the green turban on her head. Slade had made a reference to the hat earlier. The idea that had germinated at his mention of it now began to grow.

In flashback, she remembered the mailman who

stopped at the television studio practically every day for the past year. Yet when she had seen him off work in a store without his uniform, she hadn't recognized him.

The wheels began to turn inside her head. A disguise was the answer, a very subtle disguise. Lisa Talmadge had shoulder-length silver blond hair. Mrs. Ann Eldridge, whose hair had not been seen, thanks to the turban, would have—Lisa thought for an instant—red hair.

It would be a perfect foil for her fair complexion and green eyes and such a startling contrast to the true color of her pale hair. With luck, Slade Blackwell would never compare the two women.

Within seconds, Lisa was at the cash register, paying for her meal and inquiring where the closest wig shop was located. She was told a boutique three blocks away carried a small selection. In all it turned out that the shop had no more than a dozen wigs in their inventory. One was red, a shade of flaming orange, cut short, styled in a pixieish bob. Lisa hardly recognized herself when the saleswoman helped her put it on.

"That's it," she declared, and walked out of the store moments later wearing it, carrying the green turban in her hand. A brighter shade of lipstick glistened on her lips.

On the way back to the office, Lisa passed a jewelry store and remembered the "Mrs." part of her disguise. She hurried inside and bought the first inexpensive plain gold wedding band she saw. Outside the shop, she slipped off her birthstone and slipped on the wedding band.

At ten minutes past one she was rushing toward the

Blackwell office. Aware that she had taken longer than she should, she crossed her fingers and hoped that she could make it back before Slade Blackwell did.

After going through all of this, she didn't want to give him cause to dismiss her and have the agency send him someone else. Not when she hadn't accomplished her objective.

Unfortunately her wish wasn't to be. Approaching the office entrance from the opposite direction was Slade Blackwell. His long strides brought him to the door three steps before Lisa reached it. He waited for her, his dark eyes making a sweeping appraisal of her.

"I'm sorry I'm late," Lisa murmured hastily. Self-consciously she raised a hand to the red wig. She wondered if he was astute enough to recognize it as a wig. "I stopped at a salon during my lunch hour and had my hair washed and blown dry."

His gaze flicked to the green turban in her hand. There was nothing in his carved features to indicate he didn't believe her story. "Because of my comment about your hat?" he questioned, opening the door and holding it for Lisa.

"Well, yes," she admitted, glad she wasn't Pinocchio or her nose would have been six feet long by now.

The hard line of his mouth curved faintly. Lisa saw the suggestion of a smile an instant before she walked ahead of him into the office.

"I didn't intend to sound critical, Mrs. Eldridge. I was merely curious. Women so seldom wear hats nowadays," he remarked.

"I don't generally, either." Lisa Talmadge wore hats, not Ann Eldridge. She would have to remember that.

"Tell me, do you have a temper to match it?" The amusement in his low voice was unmistakable.

"Everyone has a temper, Mr. Blackwell. Some people have a lower boiling point than others," she replied. "That's the only difference."

"Is your boiling point low?" he mocked.

"Well, well, well!" The exclamation from Drew Rutledge allowed Lisa to ignore Slade Blackwell's taunting question. "If I'd had any idea your hat was hiding that hair, I would never have let you lunch alone!"

"She's married, Drew," Slade pointed out dryly, not pausing in his walk toward his own office.

"I know." Drew winked at Lisa as if there was a secret between them. "But just because she's married doesn't mean she has to eat alone or that I must deprive myself of an innocent hour of her beautiful company."

"You'll have to forgive him, Mrs. Eldridge." There was friendly indulgence in the look Slade Blackwell gave his assistant. "Drew has a weakness for redheads."

"That's right," Drew agreed as Lisa's shorter steps carried her toward the double doors Slade was holding open for her. "Slade gets the blondes and I get the redheads."

What happens when you have both in one? Lisa thought, her cheeks dimpling faintly at the unspoken question. But that was her secret and she hoped it would stay that way. She had barely walked around the desk to sit in her chair when Slade Blackwell's curt voice wiped the trace of a smile from her face.

"Haven't you finished those letters yet, Mrs.

Eldridge?" His dark gaze dwelt pointedly on the partially complete letter in the typewriter.

"Not yet," Lisa defended herself instinctively. "Shortly after you left the office, Dr—Mr. Rutledge came in to ask me for the Talmadge file. I'm not familiar with your filing system and it took me some time to find it." Another lie, since Drew had been the one to locate it, but she doubted that Slade Blackwell would ever question him about it.

"It's a standard system," he replied automatically. The hint of asperity in his tone indicated that he found her excuse inadequate. Almost instantly a preoccupied light entered his eyes. "The Talmadge file," he repeated in a thoughtful murmur.

"Yes, the Talmadge file," Lisa affirmed. "He assured me that he had your permission to take it from the files. If you want me to, I'll go and get it and bring it back." Gladly, on winged feet, she would go after it.

"That's not necessary." Slade Blackwell dismissed the suggestion without hesitation. "Get Mrs. Talmadge on the phone for me. Her number is in the directory on your desk."

"Yes, sir." Lisa hid her dismay and quickly flipped through the telephone listings until she found her aunt's number. Her pulse was hammering in her throat as she dialed it and listened to the ring.

. "Talmadge residence," Mildred answered on the fourth ring.

"One moment." She couldn't disguise the pitch of her voice, not with Slade Blackwell standing beside her desk. "Did you want to take the call here or in your office?"

"In my office." He started to turn, then stopped, his

gaze narrowing on her. "A piece of advice, Mrs. Eldridge. If encouraged, Drew will find many excuses to distract you from your work."

Lisa stiffened. "I'll remember that, Mr. Blackwell. But, as you also pointed out to Mr. Rutledge, I am married so he's unlikely to receive any encouragement from me."

"I hope not."

Fuming silently at his cynically skeptical reply, Lisa glared at the retreating set of broad shoulders as he walked to the connecting door to his inner office.

"He is insufferable!" she murmured aloud before hearing Mildred's impatient voice in the receiver. Lisa removed her hand from the mouthpiece and said huskily, "Please hold the line for a call from Mr. Blackwell."

"Slade? Well, tell him to hurry. I can't stand here all day," the housekeeper grumbled.

There was the telltale click of another phone being picked up. As Lisa replaced the receiver, she heard the echo of Slade Blackwell's voice on the line.

What did he want to talk to Mitzi about? The impulse was strong to listen in, but Lisa knew she didn't dare. She turned her swivel chair to the typewriter and picked up the earpiece for the dictaphone.

She tried desperately to concentrate on the letter she had to finish, but she kept watching the small telephone light out of the corner of her eye. Her typing was not the fastest to begin with. The distraction of watching the telephone made it even slower. It didn't improve until the light went out.

That letter was finished and another begun when the

telephone rang again; a business call for Slade. She transferred it to him and went back to the letter. She wanted them all done and ready for his signature when he asked for them, which she guessed would be soon.

Despite numerous interruptions—phone calls, clients, and instructions from Slade to make notations of appointments with various people—Lisa completed the last of the dictation an hour and a half later. She had it all stacked neatly on her desk and was looking apprehensively through the papers in the tray that needed to be filed. Any filing system was a mystery to her, whether it was a standard system as Slade had informed her, or not.

The door to his private office opened and Slade walked out. "Have you finished those letters yet, Mrs. Eldridge?" His attitude indicated that he expected a negative answer.

"They are right here, sir." Lisa wasn't able to keep the ring of triumphant satisfaction out of her voice as she gathered the papers together.

He took them from her without making a complimentary remark. As before, he skimmed through the contents as if expecting to find something to criticize. It irritated Lisa, mostly because she was afraid he would find something. Apparently satisfied with what he found, he turned and started toward his office. Pausing, his dark, impersonal gaze swung to her.

"I have dictated some legal briefs I would like typed. They are filled with 'to wits' and 'whereas' and 'parties of the first part.'" His mouth quirked, a dry humor surfacing to her surprise. "Do you think you can do them?"

The prospect of spending the rest of the afternoon pounding at the typewriter was depressing. It brought her no closer to the purpose of her masquerade. But she really had very little choice.

"I . . . can try." She smiled in an attempt to hide her lack of enthusiasm.

"Very well. I'll bring them in to you." The instant he disappeared inside his office, Lisa took a deep breath and exhaled it angrily in a sigh.

Almost as quickly, Slade was back and Lisa had to fix an interested and studious look on her face. He briefly went over the contents with her and explained the form he wanted the material to take. He was all business, very professional, yet patient with her ignorance. Grudgingly Lisa gave him credit for that. She couldn't accuse him of being a tyrannical employer.

After he'd left so she could begin typing, Lisa wished she had not taken advantage of his mistaken identity of her. It was proving to be a lot of work. Surely there must have been an easier way to get the information she was seeking. But she couldn't think of a single one as she put the paper and carbons in the typewriter.

CHAPTER THREE

A BLOCK FROM HER AUNT'S HOUSE the street was empty of cars and pedestrians. Lisa paused to pull the red wig from her head and free her blond hair from its confining pins. Stuffing the wig in her handbag, she briskly ruffled her hair to rid it of that matted look.

Some vacation, she thought wearily. Her arms, neck and shoulders ached from the unaccustomed time she had spent at the typewriter. If this was what it was like to be a secretary, she decided that she was going to recommend Donna, her production staff secretary, for a raise when she got back to the Baltimore television station.

A car turned onto the street behind her, and Lisa cast a frightened look over her shoulder. Before leaving the office, she had heard Slade Blackwell mention to Drew that he was going straight from the office to Mitzi's house. She expected him to overtake her any minute. Not this time, though, as the car drew level with her and Lisa saw the driver was a balding, middle-aged man.

But the scare prodded her into walking faster. She had to reach the house before Slade Blackwell or all her plans were for naught. The wrought-iron gates blocking the driveway entrance at the sidewalk were closed when Lisa reached the house. She didn't breathe easy until she was inside. Her plan to rush immediately to her room and change clothes was thwarted by her aunt, who appeared almost the second Lisa closed the entrance door behind her.

"You made it back without getting lost, didn't you?" Mitzi's wide smile of greeting was swiftly replaced by a look of concern. "You look exhausted, Lisa."

"It's been a long day." The muscles in her arm protested achingly as she tried to brush the hair away from her face.

"If I'd known you were going to overdo it your first day here, I would have waited till tomorrow to invite Slade for dinner. As it is, it's too late. He'll be here any minute," her aunt apologized.

"I'd better run upstairs and change, then."

"There's no need to," Mitzi insisted. "From the looks of you, you'd do better to sit down and put your feet up and maybe have a relaxing drink." It sounded like a heavenly suggestion to Lisa, even though she knew she couldn't accept it. "Besides," Mitzi continued, "the outfit you're wearing is very attractive. You don't have to change it."

But that was precisely the point. She did have to change it. Slade Blackwell had seen her in it practically all day, but Lisa couldn't very well tell her aunt that.

"I think I would rather, Mitzi. A wash and a change of clothes will make me seem like a new person." *I hope,* Lisa thought.

"You do what you think is best," her aunt conceded.

Lisa started to hurry towards the stairs. "If your Mr. Blackwell arrives before I'm down, make my apologies, will you?" she tossed over her shoulder. Pausing at the stairs, she added, "I noticed the driveway gates are closed."

"That's all right," Mitzi waved aside the comment. "Slade will probably walk. He usually does."

Suppressing a shudder that he might have been only a block or two behind her all the way from the office, Lisa darted up the stairs. As she reached her room, she heard the opening of the entrance door downstairs. Another minute and her deception would have been uncovered before she had had a chance to make it work.

Her bedroom was spacious, decorated in vivid greens and golds. An alcove of the room was designed as a mock sitting room, complete with sofa, chair and an antique secretary desk. What had once been a dressing room off the bedroom had been remodeled into a bathroom. It was to the latter that Lisa hurried.

She would have loved to take a quick shower, but there wasn't time. So she settled for washing and splashing lots of cold water on her face to rinse away the weariness. From the closet, she chose a creamy blue dress. Its simple lines flowed smoothly over the bodice to her waist before flaring into a full skirt. Its style and color made her look petite and dainty, an appearance of fragility that was deceiving and a definite contrast to the bold outfit she had worn earlier.

Reapplying her makeup, Lisa was adding the finishing touches of mascara to her lashes when she noticed the way the blue color of her dress accented the green of her eyes. Only last night Mitzi had made the comment that her eyes were Lisa's most striking feature.

Two women with the same unusual shade of green eyes would definitely be noticed by Slade Blackwell.

But how on earth could she change the color of her eyes, Lisa wondered frantically.

Breathing in sharply, she dropped the mascara wand on the dressing table and raced into the bedroom proper. Her bag was on the bed where she had left it. Lisa opened it and dumped the contents, wig and all, onto the bedspread, scattering them around until she found her sunglasses.

Quickly she slipped on the large, wrap-around glasses and dashed back to the mirror. The lenses didn't conceal her eyes with the reflecting ability of some mirrorlike sunglasses, but the smoky-blue tint did mask the color of her eyes.

"Praise be," Lisa murmured in satisfaction.

Dressed and with every potential problem countered, she had no more reason to linger in her room. At the top of the stairs she hesitated, hearing the low voices coming from the living room. She pressed a hand against her jittery stomach, trying to quiet the butterfly sensation.

Her palms were clammy with nervousness. She couldn't put off the moment of truth. Fighting the traitorous weakness in her knees, she descended the stairs and entered the living room.

"There you are, Lisa. I—" Mitzi's bright exclamation ended abruptly as a frown dressed her forehead. Lisa was conscious of Slade Blackwell courteously rising to meet her, but she kept her attention on her aunt. "Why are you wearing sunglasses at this hour?" Mitzi queried with astonishment.

"Working so much of the time in the television studio around all those bright lights, my eyes have become sensitive to too much light. After being in the sun all day, my eyes started to bother me." Lisa was becoming certain she was a natural-born liar. "A specialist recommended that I wear sunglasses whenever that happened."

"You never mentioned it," her aunt queried.

"It isn't a serious problem. More of an inconvenience than anything," Lisa assured her, and turned to meet Slade Blackwell. She had been covertly watching him ever since she entered the room, but she had not detected any glimmer of recognition of her as Ann Eldridge in his dark gaze. "You must be Slade Blackwell." A full smile parted her lips as she walked toward him, extending a hand in greeting. "I'm Lisa Talmadge, Mitzi's niece."

"So I guessed." He returned her smile with one of his own.

The warmth it gave to his hard features was astounding. It seemed to slowly draw her breath away. Lisa realized how very potent his charm could be when he turned it on, as he was doing now. Her hand was lost in the firm grip of his, being held longer than was necessary. It created a disturbing sensation in the pit of her stomach.

"Mitzi described you perfectly as a beautiful, intelligent blonde, but she didn't mention that you had cold hands," he mocked, the velvet quality of his voice taking any sting from his comment.

"Cold hands, warm heart," her aunt quipped from the side.

"I think it's a sign of poor circulation," Lisa denied her aunt's allegation, and determinedly withdrew her hand from his warm grasp.

She had feld herself beginning to warm to him.

Seeing this side of him, she could well understand how her aunt, who was so sentimental and romantic, had been taken in by Slade Blackwell's charm. The secret, Lisa believed, was to stay out of range of that magnetic forcefield radiating around him. His physical attraction was a bit overwhelming at close quarters.

That was something she hadn't noticed about him at the office where Slade Blackwell had kept himself aloof and impersonal, crisply professional except for that one taunting remark about her red hair. Correction—Ann Eldridge's red hair.

"May I fix you a drink, Lisa?" Slade Blackwell asked smoothly, not faltering even slightly over the use of her given name.

"Lisa drinks gin," Mitzi Talmadge inserted, turning to Lisa to add, "Slade has a bartender's touch with mixed drinks."

"Gin?" Slade looked at her, waiting for a confirmation of her choice.

"No, I think I'll just have some juice." As tired as she was, Lisa knew the last thing she needed was an alcoholic beverage to muddle her thinking.

"Are you sure?" He gave her a chance to change her mind.

"Quite sure," Lisa nodded positively.

He walked to an ornate wooden trolley cart that was used as a serving bar. "There's tomato and orange juice in the icebox," he said without looking. "Which would you prefer?"

"Tomato." Lisa watched him pour the tomato juice over the ice cubes in a glass, add a dash of tabasco sauce and a wedge of lemon. Never once did he falter over the location of an item. "You know where every-thing is, don't you?" she commented, letting an inflec-tion of sarcasm creep into her voice.

"I drop in quite often." He shrugged offhandedly, carrying her drink to her, but his dark gaze was probing her expression for the reason she had used that tone.

"But not often enough to wear out your welcome." Her tongue seemed to be running away with her, maybe because she had held it in all day.

"I hope not." But this time his smile didn't reach his eyes, eyes that had gone blank and shuttered.

"You couldn't possibly do that, Slade," Mitzi laughed, missing or overlooking the tiny barbs in Lisa's remarks. "Mildred and I love having you here. You couldn't come often enough. I would be delighted if you looked on this as your second home. You should. After all, you're responsible—directly and indirectly—for all that's been done here."

"Of course, how could I have forgotten?" The words were out before Lisa could check them.

She seemed bent on a course of self-destruction, making Slade an enemy and arousing his suspicions. Maybe it was true that those who do wrong really want to be caught.

Lisa only knew she had gone too far to reverse direction now. "Mitzi told me that you persuaded her to reopen the house and supervised the remodeling and redecorating. Naturally you would be familiar with everything, wouldn't you?"

"A house in this neighborhood of Old Charleston is an investment. Besides, it would have been a shame to

let this beautiful home become a derelict of the past," ·
Slade replied.

"I agree with you completely," said Mitzi. "In fact I
did the first time you suggested it, Slade, but I would
never have attempted it on my own. Not that I couldn't
have done it, but it's so time-consuming. You know
how I dislike details, Lisa," she laughed at herself. "If
Slade hadn't intervened to take charge of the workmen
and various trades, I doubt if I would have fixed the
old place up simply because I don't like the hassle
that's inevitable."

"Yes," Lisa agreed. "You were lucky to have Slade
take care of all that." She turned to him, a saccharine
smile curving her mouth. "Ever since Mitzi has moved
back to Charleston, all her letters have been singing
your praises. You've become quite indispensable to
her."

"I think Mitzi and I have become good friends. The
purpose of friendship is to help each other when help is
needed." There was a challenging set to his jaw
although his voice remained quite calm and steady.
"Now that Mitzi's on her own, without a man to look
after her, I try to do what I can to help."

"I'm sure you do," Lisa taunted softly, and his gaze
narrowed with piercing thoughtfulness.

"Believe me, I appreciate it," Mitzi stated. "I'm not
interested in business and finances. I don't want to be
bothered with investment credits and capital gains and
stock dividends. It's a relief to turn it all over to Slade.
I'm afraid I've rather taken advantage of his good
nature, though."

"It must be wonderful to have someone you can

trust so implicitly." Lisa thought the real point was who was taking advantage of whom? "It must be an awesome responsibility for you . . . Slade—" she hesitated a bare second over his Christian name "—to have virtually sole control of someone else's money."

"Yes, it is," he agreed.

Lisa saw his mouth tighten and knew her gibes had to be getting close to their mark. She really should keep quiet, but she was deriving such fiendish delight out of antagonizing him.

Her subconscious seemed to have come up with a daring battle plan. While Lisa Talmadge attacked him boldly headon, Ann Eldridge could sneak up on him from behind.

"Lisa thinks I'm too trusting," Mitzi sighed in amusement. "But I'd rather be that way than the reverse. And of course, she doesn't know you as I do."

The invisible darts Lisa had been tossing hadn't escaped her aunt's attention. Neither did she seem upset by them. Yet, in the acknowledgment, there was a hint for a truce, however temporary.

"You're too trusting," Lisa reaffirmed, but gently and with affection. "It would be too easy for someone you like to take advantage of you."

Her subtle accusation against Slade Blackwell had been made, but not in a way that he could take open offense. He didn't like it—Lisa could tell by the hardening of his dark features.

"May I fix you another drink, Mitzi?" Slade rose from his chair, carrying his emptied glass.

"I don't believe so." Mitzi swirled her drink, ice cubes clinking against the side with the agitation of the liquid. "I still have some left, but help yourself by all means."

"I think I will," he said grimly, walking to the trolley cart. "In one way or another, it's been a long, tiring day."

You can say that again, Lisa thought, remembering the chaos in the office that afternoon.

The telephone had hardly ever stopped ringing, and clients kept stopping in expecting to talk to Slade whether they had appointments or not. It had taken forever to finish typing those letters, or so it seemed. The legal briefs weren't even half-completed.

"I never did have a chance to ask you how your day was, Lisa," Mitzi turned to her, curious and interested. "You left a message with Mildred that you were going to visit some friends. Did they take you sightseeing?"

"We were going to go after lunch," Lisa lied again, "but we got to talking. One thing led to another and before I knew it the afternoon was gone."

"I wasn't aware that you had friends living here in Charleston," Slade commented.

"College chums," Mitzi inserted.

"Yes, Susan, Peg and I were roommates in college." Lisa hoped that wherever they were, they didn't mind her using them in her story. "We're planning to make a day of it tomorrow since they're on vacation, too," she said, establishing a reason for her absence tomorrow.

"You must invite them over some time. I'd like to meet them," her aunt suggested.

"I'll do that," Lisa smiled. What else could she say?

From the archway came the sound of someone clearing her throat to attract attention, and Lisa glanced over her shoulder to see the unsmiling face of the housekeeper framed in the opening.

"If you'd all come into the dining room, I'll dish up the soup," she announced gruffly.

"We're coming," Mitzi agreed, and Slade was at the older woman's side when she rose from her chair.

"Did you fix my favorite, Mildred?" There was a teasing lightness to Slade's question.

Lisa was surprised to see the housekeeper flustered by his inquiry. There was a definite pink in her cheeks, which she tried to hide by turning away.

"It's she-crab soup, if that's what you're asking," she retorted.

Not only was her aunt under his spell, Lisa realized, but the housekeeper was as well. Lisa had not thought anything or anyone could pierce that armor of weary indifference that Mildred wore. The more she thought about it, as they followed the housekeeper into the dining room, the more logical it became that Slade Blackwell should cultivate the housekeeper's affection. Plus Slade was the one who had hired Mildred. She would naturally feel a certain sense of obligation and loyalty to him for obtaining this position. He would want an ally in the household to keep him informed. Mildred was being used as surely as her aunt was. The man was completely without scruples. But Lisa was determined that things were not going to go his way any longer.

The dining room was a formal, yet comfortable room. There were three accesses to the room: a set of double doors that opened into the living room; another set opening into the hallway; and a third door to the kitchen. The rich luster of the woodwork and furniture was enhanced by the subtle pattern of the embossed wallpaper, a shade of peach. The crystal teardrops of the chandelier cast refracted light rays on the high beamed ceiling.

The leaves had been removed from the carved oak table to seat the three of them comfortably without a long stretch of white linen tablecloth to separate them. As Slade courteously held out the chair at the head of the table for Mitzi, Lisa walked around them to sit on her aunt's right.

Reaching for the carved wood of the chair back, her hand instead touched the back of his. Lisa drew it back in surprise, as if encountering a hot flame. Slade was directly behind her, an arm curved around to pull out the chair for her. She glanced at him, his dark eyes taunting, and an inner radar system seemed to clang in alarm at his closeness.

A built-in defense mechanism made Lisa step quickly aside to elude the force of his male presence. "Thank you," she murmured tightly as he held out the chair for her. Her shoulders felt the brush of his hard fingers through the thin material of her dress, her nerve ends quivering in reaction.

It was purely a physical response, regardless of the fact that she disliked him intensely. Lisa recognized that and hoped that forewarned was to be forearmed. She had never been accused of being a prude. She was well aware that she possessed a passionate nature.

In the past, she had met men she found physically attractive but for one reason or another had not liked personally, and she had always managed to control her reactions. She could do it again. She would not be ensnared by his sex appeal and lose sight of what he was as a man.

He was seated across the table from her, and she realized she had been staring at him quite openly, a fact he was well aware of as he watched her with masked alertness. For a panicked second, Lisa thought he could tell what she had been thinking. More than once she had been informed that her expressive green eyes revealed what she was thinking and feeling. Stormy green when she was angry, sparkling with a million tiny lights when she was happy, a murky green when she was troubled, a mysterious clear green when she was fascinated with something or attracted to someone.

But that wasn't the case this time, she remembered thankfully. The smoke blue sunglasses hid her thoughts. He didn't know of her vulnerability to him physically. But it was something Ann Eldridge would have to watch, since she didn't have the benefit of sunglasses.

"You were saying you had a rough day at the office, Slade," Mitzi commented, making the opening gambit of table conversation. "You were busy?"

"No more so than usual," he replied, and Lisa didn't think that augured well for tomorrow. "It's just that both Bob and Mary Lou are gone, which puts an extra workload on the rest of us."

"Vacation?" Mitzi leaned back in her chair as an unhurried Mildred began serving the aromatically steaming cups of soup.

"No, Mary Lou's parents were in an auto accident,"

Slade explained. "Her father was killed outright and her mother is in very serious condition in the hospital. So I'm stuck with a temporary girl as my secretary, which louses up the office routine even more."

"That's hardly her fault." Lisa instinctively defended her own inadequacies in the position.

"I didn't say that it was her fault," he corrected with dry sharpness. "But it would have been considerably easier on all of us if I could have obtained some trained help instead of this secretary who's virtually a novice."

"Trained help?" Lisa bridled at the term. "You make it sound as if she's supposed to be a trained dog that jumps through hoops on your command. You should give her credit for doing the very best she can."

A dark brow quirked in arrogant speculation. "Are you always so quick to defend people you've never met?"

Lisa realized she had been too vocal in her defense of the supposedly unknown secretary. She quickly dipped her spoon in the soup to conceal the intensity of her interest.

"Let's just say that I always support the underdog, especially if she's a woman." But the words came out sharp and argumentative despite her desire to sound casual and offhand.

"Are you one of those feminists?" There was dry laughter in his voice and the glitter of mockery in his eyes.

Stiffening, Lisa returned his look coldly. "Are you one of those chauvinists?"

"I guess it was too much to hope for that you two wouldn't clash," Mitzi sighed, glancing from one to the other. Her expression was a mixture of regret and amusement.

"We aren't clashing, exactly." Lisa regretted her challenging outburst, but only because it had been issued in front of her aunt. "We simply have different points of view."

"Perhaps not as different as you think." His tone suggested some mysterious message that Lisa was supposed to understand, but she didn't.

And she said so. "I don't think that's true."

"You indicated that you don't believe I'm giving this temporary girl a chance, when the opposite is true, especially if she continues to show a willingness to learn. But I certainly can't be blamed for saying that it's inconvenient in the meantime to have inexperienced help," Slade concluded, so reasonably that it set Lisa's teeth on edge.

Lisa doubted that he really meant a single word he said and had only made the remark for Mitzi's benefit. Chameleonlike, he would change his stand on anything to one that her aunt would approve.

"Tell me about Mary Lou's replacement," Mitzi requested, "What is she like? She seems to have impressed you even though you claim she's a novice."

"She's young." His gaze flicked briefly to Lisa, and she held her breath, knowing he was making a fleeting comparison between herself and her alter ego, Ann Eldridge. "In her early twenties, about Lisa's age, I would guess. She has bright red hair, very attractive and eyes the color of—"

"Isn't that typical?" Lisa rushed to interrupt him, fearful Mitzi would make a comment about her own green eyes if Slade mentioned Ann's. "You ask a man to describe a woman and immediately he gives a physical description, judging a woman on her looks instead of her ability. They'll forgive a lack of brains if a woman is beautiful."

"Lisa!" her aunt admonished softly.

"That's quite all right, Mitzi. I understand what Lisa is saying." Slade dismissed the need for reproof. The look he gave Lisa was one of an adult indulging in the temper tantrum of a child, which did little to improve her disposition. "This new secretary happens to have brains as well as beauty. The reason I didn't boast about her skills is because she doesn't have any. I would be surprised if she can type thirty-five words a minute."

"Then why keep her on?" Lisa challenged. It was pure bravado since she might be providing him with the thought of firing Ann Eldridge and that would be cutting her own throat.

"Because she has a remarkable ability to handle several things at once without ever becoming distracted or flustered. That's a valuable asset," he stated. "When Mary Lou does return, she'll probably have a backlog of correspondence to type, but at least I don't have to be out there holding the new girl's hand."

"If she's as attractive as you say," Mitzi teased, "maybe that's unfortunate."

"Sorry," Slade smiled, "but she's married. Very happily, I understand."

"That's a pity," her aunt responded. "It sounds as if that was one girl who might have kept up with your many and varied interests."

"I guess that's something I won't find out." He shrugged. "How's the new novel coming along?"

"Marvelously!" her aunt declared enthusiastically, and the topic of conversation was switched.

As far as Lisa was concerned, the dinner was spoiled by Slade's presence. She took little part in the discussion, a fact that Mitzi didn't seem to notice as she warmed to the subject of her latest book. Slade pretended to concentrate on what her aunt was saying, but Lisa was intensely conscious of how often his piercing gaze was focused on her. It was disconcerting, like being under a microscope.

"Mildred, we'll have our coffee in the living room," Mitzi informed the housekeeper when they had finished dessert. "That way Slade can add a little brandy to his." She laughed briefly, and changed the subject, hardly drawing a breath in the transition.

"I wanted to show you the review of my latest book, too. It's in my study."

"I'll get it for you," Lisa volunteered quickly, eager for a few minutes alone.

"Would you mind?" The absent question by Mitzi was answered by a shake of Lisa's head. "It's in the pile of papers on the right-hand side of my desk. Somewhere in the middle, I think."

"I'll find it," she assured her aunt, hastily retreating while Mitzi and Slade started for the living room.

Study was a loose term since there wasn't anything about the room that resembled a study with the exception of the abundance of books. In this room, the creative side of Mitzi's personality surfaced amidst a clutter of papers, notes, books and magazines.

Yet it was definitely a feminine room, painted a bright, cheery yellow. A flowered sofa repeated the color. In a corner by a window sat a small, round table, painted white with a white cane-backed chair beside it. It was where Mitzi had her coffee and noon lunches.

There were no shelves of books, as such. They were stacked in every corner and scattered on every piece of furniture along with scraps of paper. A typewriter was on a long counter-style table. The table's surface was buried beneath papers, pencils, carbons and more books. There was a desk in the room, but its use seemed to be confined to being a catchall for more material.

There were three stacks of papers in all shapes and sizes on the right-hand side of the desk. Naturally Lisa found the newspaper clipping in the last stack she went through. Restoring the stack to its former ordered disorder, she turned to leave.

The study door opened as she made her turn and Slade walked in. For an instant, Lisa was too surprised to react. She stood in front of the desk, holding the paper and staring.

The click of the door latch closing seemed to suddenly isolate them from the rest of the house. Her pulse rocketed in alarm. The muscles of her throat constricted and she couldn't speak as he pinned her with his gaze.

"Did Mitzi send you in here?" She swallowed tightly, not certain why she was afraid.

"No, I came on my own." There was hardly a crack in his granite-hard features as he spoke.

"There was no need." Lisa raised her chin in a

gesture of defiance, her shattered poise beginning to piece itself together. "I found the clipping finally."

"So I see," Slade nodded, his gaze darting indifferently to the paper clutched in her hand.

A nervous hesitation quivered through her in the ensuing silence. There was something ominous in the crackling tension that made her doubly uneasy.

"Now that I've found it, I'd better take it in to Mitzi." Lisa realized she was rattling on like a clucking chicken, but she couldn't help herself.

Slade stood in front of the door, barring her way, but Lisa took a step forward anyway, expecting him to open the door for her. He didn't move.

"You aren't leaving yet," he told her in no uncertain terms.

Lisa stopped short. "What do you mean?" she breathed, caught between anger and dread.

"You are not leaving until you explain to me what's going on," he stated.

And Lisa felt a cold chill dancing down her spine. She had thought she had fooled him, that he hadn't recognized that she and Ann Eldridge were one and the same person. But obviously she had been kidding herself. She had underestimated him. How foolish! And how dangerous.

CHAPTER FOUR

PALING, LISA FELT the confidence draining from her as rapidly as the color receded from her face. Slade Blackwell had seen through her ruse. If only she had seen the file, obtained some proof to back up her suspicions. As it was, she had nothing with which to confront him. And how could she explain the deception?

"What's going on?" she repeated with false blankness.

"That's right." The line of his mouth was thin, harsh and forbidding.

"I don't think I know what you mean," Lisa stalled.

"Don't you?" Slade taunted with arrogant challenge.

A step in front of the door, he had not moved since entering the study. Yet he seemed to fill the room, intimidating Lisa until her legs felt like two quivering sticks of jelly. She wanted to sink into the nearest chair and confess her misdeed. But that would be too much like admitting guilt when he was the unscrupulous one who should feel guilty.

"Your question is confusing." Why was her lying tongue failing her now? "What's going on where?"

At his step forward, Lisa wanted to retreat. She had the eerie sensation of being stalked, but the large desk was directly behind her. There wasn't anywhere to run even if she could make her legs move.

"Your pretended innocence isn't fooling me, Lisa." His voice was smooth and controlled. She wished for a measure of his calmness. "I dislike people who sneak around."

Lowering her chin, she stared at her hands and the fluttering paper in the trembling fingers. "Sneak around?" She swallowed to rid her voice of its betraying tremor. "How could I be accused of sneaking around? Mitzi sent me in here."

"You know damned well that's not what I mean." Despite the imprecation, his tone of voice didn't change.

"Then you'll have to be more explicit with your questions." Lifting her head to challenge him boldly, Lisa clung to her false ignorance, hoping her racing brain would come up with a plausible reason for her deception—a reason other than the truth. "I'm at a complete loss to understand your meaning."

His gaze narrowed, impaling Lisa on its thrusting point. "I'll make myself clearer. Mitzi may believe that nonsense about personalities clashing and chemistries being wrong, but I don't buy it."

Lisa breathed in sharply. He didn't know! He didn't know she was Ann Eldridge! The knowledge sang through her veins, warming her with victory. She wanted to laugh wildly with delight.

"You don't?" she drawled. A suggestion of dimples dented her cheeks as she tried to conceal the bubbling smile tickling her mouth.

"No, I don't," Slade answered flatly. "I believe in neither love at first sight nor hatred at first sight. And your dislike of me borders on hatred, even though you've just met me."

"Hatred is a harsh word." Lisa was brimming with confidence now.

"It's a harsh emotion," he retorted. "You've been sniping at me all evening, and I want to know why."

Lisa's battle plan called for a frontal attack. She took a deep breath and plunged forward. "It's very simple. Unlike my aunt, I don't trust you."

His jaw hardened. "You made that obvious to Mitzi."

"Did I? Good." A smile accompanied the honey-coated comment.

"What's your game?" His dark head was tipped to the side, the angular planes of his face severely controlled to remain expressionless and cold.

"My game?" A delicate winged brow arched above the frame of her sunglasses. The question momentarily threw her off balance. "You ask *me* that?"

"Don't look so indignant, Lisa." One corner of his mouth curled upward in a jeer. "It isn't convincing."

Her temper flared. "And your apparent interest and concern for Mitzi is downright sickening," she seethed. "She must have seemed easy prey for you—divorced, alone, seemingly without any close relatives. And let's not leave out wealthy! You could even claim old family ties."

"The key word here is wealthy, isn't it?" he mused.

Her anger didn't seem to worry him. Slade was closer now, looming in front of her. His height seemed to dwarf her, forcing her to tilt her head back to meet the black glitter of his gaze. Warily she was conscious of his muscular physique and the blatant virility that was such an overwhelming part of him.

"Yes," she agreed, "the key word here is wealthy.

You've gone to great lengths to make yourself indispensable to Mitzi. You must be laughing up your sleeve at how gullible she is!"

"Are you?"

Slade Blackwell was clever. Lisa knew it would take a great deal to provoke him into admitting anything. But she could be cunning, too. Hadn't she already fooled him once?

"I don't find it at all funny!" she retorted. "She trusts you, and you're stealing her blind. It must be a rude awakening for you to discover that she isn't quite as alone in the world as you thought. Regardless of the fact that she and my uncle were divorced, my parents and I still think of her as part of our family. And we're certainly not going to let some cheap, money-grubbing lawyer take advantage of her!"

"Oh?" Slade seemed coldly amused by her threat. "What are you going to do about it?"

"I'm going to make her see what a conniving thief you are," she declared angrily.

"Then what?" He eyed her steadily, obviously confident that she wouldn't succeed, but he didn't know about Ann Eldridge.

"What do you mean?" Lisa frowned, not seeing the relevance of his question.

"What are you going to get out of it?" he elucidated calmly.

"The satisfaction of Mitzi seeing you for what you really are," she retorted.

"That's all?" Slade smiled with arrogant skepticism.

"What do you mean?" She was beginning to feel like a broken record, but she was puzzled by his attitude.

"You seem intent on getting me out of Mitzi's life

and her affairs," he replied. "Would that be because once I'm gone, you can step in?"

Lisa tensed, reading the implication he had intended her to find. "What are you getting at?" she demanded.

"That you aren't any blood relation to her. She has none left." His sharp gaze never left her face. "Admittedly you're her favorite niece, but the relationship is based on a marriage that has since been terminated."

"That's only a technicality." She defended her status in the household.

"My profession deals in technicalities," Slade reminded her with a trace of sardonicism. "Another interesting fact is that Mitzi has lived in Charleston for several years now, yet this is the first visit you've made."

"It's the first chance I've had to come," Lisa argued.

"Or the first time you thought there was reason?" he countered.

"Reason?" She drew herself up to her full height that still left her several inches shorter than Slade. "What are you saying?"

"That your motive for being here isn't as pure and lily white as you pretend." His gaze raked her with sweeping disdain.

"My motive?" Lisa repeated incredulously.

"It seems to me that you scheduled this visit after you became aware of how often my name was mentioned in your aunt's letters. Until then, I think you were too certain of Mitzi's affection for you to bother about visiting an elderly relative when you could be having fun with friends your own age. Money brought you here, Lisa Talmadge, Mitzi's money," he concluded.

"Are you accusing me of—" Lisa began in outraged anger.

"I'm saying that you dislike me because Mitzi had turned to me for advice in money matters and you see that as a threat, not to Mitzi but to yourself." Slade studied her with contempt.

"That's absurd!" Lisa bristled. "I don't care what Mitzi does with her money or who she gives it to! I certainly don't expect to receive a dime of it!"

"How very nobly spoken," he taunted. "Mitzi is fond enough of you to believe that. Personally I find it pathetically phony—as false as your concern for Mitzi's welfare."

Incensed, Lisa reacted blindly, words failing her. Her palm swung in a lightning arc, striking a leanly hollowed cheek with a resounding slap. His face was as hard and unyielding as it looked, and her hand tingled painfully from the impact.

But she didn't have time to dwell on it. She was too aware of the primitive anger darkening his features. She doubted if anyone had slapped his face in a long while, especially a woman.

A deadly silence filled the room. Lisa could hear the wild racing of her pulse pounding in her ears. Her hand had left a pale imprint on his tanned cheek, and the proud flare of his nostrils said it was a mark that would not go unpunished.

"I have never hit a woman in my life." His voice was a low, savagely growling sound, drawn through teeth clenched in anger. "But you're sorely tempting me to change that."

"Don't let the fact that I'm a woman stop you," Lisa bluffed recklessly.

An ominous fire blazed in his eyes. He seemed to move closer to her and she took a hasty step backward, bumping sharply into the desk. Thrown off balance, she wavered unsteadily for a second. Before she could regain her equilibrium on her own, steel fingers had clamped around her elbow to steady her.

"Take your hand off me!" Ice dripped from her voice.

Only after she had spoken did Lisa realize that his supporting hand had been an instinctive reaction on his part. Slade would have released her instantly if she hadn't demanded it. She tried to twist free.

"Let go of me!" This time there was a trace of desperate anger in her demand.

She struck at him again with her free hand, but this he was prepared, capturing her wrist and yanking her roughly against his granite length. Strong fingers wound around a handful of silver blond hair, tugging at her tender scalp.

Lisa breathed in sharply with pain. It was the last movement she was permitted as his mouth crushed her lips. Her arms were trapped uselessly between their bodies, unable to wedge even the slightest space, his strength easily overpowering hers. Lisa reeled under the bruising pressure of his mouth.

The touch, smell and taste of him was a physical assault on her senses. Her mind could register nothing but his complete domination, making a response as impossible as resistance. She was certain the fierce mastery could continue forever, that she would be locked eternally in the steel embrace of his arms. The very instant the thought crossed her mind that she would be endlessly condemned to this punishment, the brutal force smothering her mouth was retracted.

Numbed and without strength, she couldn't move. The hand pulling at her hair no longer forced her head back, but she couldn't raise it upright. As the constricting band around her relaxed its hold, her hands clutched at the sleeves of his suit jacket for support, feeling the fluid steel **of** his muscles rippling beneath the material.

With an effort, Lisa opened her eyes to gaze at him through the smoke blue lenses of her sunglasses. Dark, ruthless male features filled her vision. There was only one weapon left that she possessed in any appreciable amounts, and she resorted to it, however ineffectual it might turn out to be.

"Is your male ego satisfied?" Her voice was unbelievably husky, trembling as violently as she was inside. "Or did you intend to rape me?"

The hand that had been at the back of her hair slid to the side of her neck. The body heat it emanated burned her sensitive flesh as his thumb roughly trailed from the point of her chin to the hollow of her throat. It pressed lightly on her windpipe as if Slade was considering strangling her.

"If that's what I intended, you wouldn't still be standing up," he said grimly.

There was a smudge of dusty-pink lipstick at the corner of his mouth, the only evidence she could see in the hard, male features that Slade had been the one to administer the punishing kiss. Lisa felt branded by it.

Her lips throbbed, her smooth skin rasped by the

faint stubble of his beard, barely noticeable by sight, but definitely by touch. Her heart was pulsing chaotically, her cheeks flushed.

"Will you please let me go?" she requested tightly.

"Not until we come to an understanding," Slade answered unequivocally.

"An understanding?" she repeated angrily, and tried to push away from his chest, but he simply tightened his hold. "I'll make no bargain with you!"

"You'll make one and like it," he snapped. "I'm going to say this once and only once. You're going to keep your nose out of things that don't concern you—and that includes Mitzi's life!"

"Her life concerns me," Lisa protested.

"All you are is her nice little niece from Baltimore. Keep it that way."

"While you keep stealing her money—not a chance!" she retorted.

"I—" But Slade didn't have a chance to finish what he was going to say. Three light raps sounded in swift succession was warning only a second before the study door opened and Mitzi's dark head peered around the door.

"You two have been in here so long I was certain you'd gotten into a scrap and needed a referee," she said. Slade was slow in releasing Lisa, despite her angry attempt to twist free. A knowing smile spread across her aunt's face. "But it wasn't that kind of a scrap that you got into."

"Yes, it was." Lisa fired a venomous look at his unruffled exterior, trembling with violent hatred. "Your Slade Blackwell was molesting me, Mitzi."

He glanced at Mitzi and drawled lazily, a hand lifting to the cheek Lisa had slapped, "I kissed her, but only after she'd practically invited me to do it."

"What he means is I slapped him," Lisa translated.

"For heaven's sake, why?" Mitzi laughed, not entirely sure how much of what was being said was the truth and how much playful exaggeration.

"Because—" Lisa began.

"Because I was criticizing her for letting so much time go by without visiting you," Slade inserted swiftly. "But it really wasn't my place to say anything, and I apologize." He turned to Lisa, his dark eyes offering a silent challenge. "That's about what happened, isn't it? Or did you want to add something?"

He was daring her to accuse him of stealing her aunt's money. But it was something Lisa wouldn't do, not until she had some proof to back up her claim.

"I can't think of anything that needs to be added," she agreed. "Not for the time being."

There was a complacent twist to his mouth. "You have quite a niece, Mitzi. She's really very stimulating. I think she intends to keep me on my toes while she's here."

"I intend to try," Lisa retorted. The review clipping had fallen to the floor. She stooped to pick it up and walked to her aunt. "I'm afraid the clipping is a little bit worse for the wear. It was caught in the middle of our confrontation."

"It's a little wrinkled," Mitzi agreed, smoothing the paper in her hand, "but not hurt. The coffee is still in the living room if you two are still interested."

Slade pushed aside the cuff of his jacket to glance at his watch. "It's getting late for me. But to show you how much I enjoyed the dinner and the company tonight, I'd like to return the hospitality by taking you and Lisa to dinner tomorrow night. If you're free, of course," he added mockingly.

"I'm never free where you're concerned," Lisa snapped.

Without blinking an eye, Slade faced her. "Then how much will it cost me?"

"You know very well that's not what I meant!" Lisa flashed, and longed to slap that complacent look from his face.

"Then you are free?" he taunted.

"But not easy." If he seemed to be determined to issue innuendoes, so would she.

"It's rare that anything worthwhile is easy." The look on his saturnine features seemed to take up the challenge she had inadvertently made.

Lisa had to clamp her mouth tightly shut to keep from telling him exactly what she thought of his chances. There had been enough arguing in front of Mitzi. The time for taking a stand against Slade Blackwell hadn't come, not until she had something to back up her suspicions.

"It's settled, then." Slade turned back to Mitzi. "Dinner tomorrow evening. I'll pick the two of you up at seven."

"No!" Lisa snapped, and received a piercing look of inquiry from him.

"She's just being stubborn." Mitzi seemed to be amused by their cutting byplay. "Of course we'll have dinner with you, Slade. I want Lisa to have a few nights out in Charleston while she's here and you know all the good places."

"No," she refused again.

"Lisa," Mitzi said in a cajoling voice.

The tiredness of Lisa's bones and muscles was making her doubly irritable. She felt at her wits' end trying to cope with this intolerable situation.

Slade must have sensed that she didn't want to bring everything out in the open yet and was backing her into a corner. Tomorrow was going to be another trying day, and she simply couldn't face the thought of seeing him tomorrow night.

"Mitzi, I'm going to be out all day tomorrow with Peg and Susan," she reasoned. "I'm not going to feel like going out tomorrow night."

"We'll make it Thursday, the day after," Slade suggested.

"Yes." By then, Lisa intended to have all the information she needed to convict Slade Blackwell beyond Mitzi's reasonable doubt.

"I'll look forward to it," he said with a maddening smile, and took his leave.

"He's an infuriating man." Lisa muttered as the study door closed behind the arrogant set of his shoulders.

"But he is a man," Mitzi observed with a bright twinkle in her eye. "If I were your age—"

"If you were my age, you'd be welcome to him." She turned away from the door to face her aunt. Her lips still felt tender from his bruising kiss. "I told you once that I don't care for the strong, masterful type. He leaves me cold."

"Cold?" Mitzi raised an eyebrow, amusement evident in the action. "I think hot is more like it."

"Please, Mitzi." Lisa lifted a warning hand of protest. "At the moment, Slade Blackwell is a very volatile subject as far as I'm concerned. And unless you want me to explode, you'd better drop it."

There was a heavy sigh of agreement from her aunt. Lisa knew she was hurt by the veiled animosity between two people she liked, but she also knew that Mitzi was going to be even more hurt when she found out the kind of man Slade Blackwell really was. In the long run it would be best, though.

Mitzi wisely didn't introduce Slade's name into the conversation again. Despite that, neither the incident in the study nor the man himself was far from Lisa's thoughts.

By ten o'clock a mental and physical exhaustion began to set in. Lisa was grateful when Mitzi suggested that it was time they went to bed. Upstairs in her room, Lisa ignored the bed in favor of the bathroom where the shower spray massaged the aching muscles of her shoulders and neck. She tumbled into bed and turned off the light. In the darkness, she wondered if thoughts of Slade and how she would unmask him, would keep her awake. That was the last thing Lisa remembered thinking.

THE STUDY DOOR WAS OPEN when Lisa came down the spiral staircase a little after seven the next morning. The typewriter was silent.

"Is that you, Lisa?" her aunt called and appeared in the doorway an instant later. "Gracious, but you are up early this morning. And all dressed, too."

"I decided that I didn't want to sleep my vacation away," Lisa lied, preferring to be snugly asleep in her canopied bed.

"Come in and join me for coffee. Mildred just brought me a fresh pot," Mitzi invited.

"I wouldn't want to disturb you. I know you're working." Her finger clutched her large purse, its sides bulging with the red wig she had crammed inside.

"Nonsense. You aren't disturbing me," her aunt insisted. "I was just taking a break before I began the next scene."

"I'd love to have coffee with you, but I'm afraid I can't." Lisa glanced at her watch. The minutes were ticking away. She needed the early start to work so she could make the transformation into Ann Eldridge before reaching Slade's office.

"Are you going somewhere at this hour?" Mitzi frowned in astonishment.

Poor Peggy and Susan, Lisa thought, they might never know how useful they had been to her since she arrived in Charleston.

"I'm meeting Sue and Peg for breakfast." She hated deceiving her aunt this way, but it was for her own good. "Since we didn't get any sight-seeing done yesterday, we thought we'd get an early start at it today."

"Oh, I see." But something in Mitzi's tone indicated that she thought they had taken leave of their senses. "What are you planning to see today? There is a tour boat that takes you to Fort Sumter where the first battle of the Civil War took place. It's really quite fascinating to wander about the old battlements and listen to the park ranger explain about the long Union seige of the fort. The South never lost it in battle. They ultimately abandoned it toward the close of the war, but it was never taken from them."

"Actually I'm not sure where we're going today," Lisa explained. "The girls know their way around better than I do, so they are making all the plans."

"Be sure to have them take you to Fort Sumter."

"I'll tell them," she promised with fingers mentally crossed. "I'd really better be going, Mitzi. I'll see you tonight."

"Have fun."

"I will," she returned and nearly dashed out the door.

Her heels clicked loudly on the paved sidewalk as she hurried along the street. At least this time she wouldn't have to stop to ask directions to Slade's office. Lisa glanced at her watch. It was nearly seven-thirty. She quickened her pace.

Using the ladies' room of a restaurant to change, she donned the flame-colored wig, outlined her lips with a coral gloss and replaced her birthstone with the wedding band. She smiled secretly to herself as she emerged, wondering if anyone had noticed the blonde going in and the redhead coming out.

When Slade arrived at the office, she was hard at work, busily transcribing the legal briefs from the dictaphone. Nodding an indifferent "good morning," he picked up the few phone messages from her desk and went directly into his own office. Lisa hoped that he hibernated there. Now that he had met Lisa Talmadge, she didn't want him noticing similarities to Ann Eldridge.

At each sound coming from the outer reception area, Lisa glanced expectantly toward the door. Drew was supposed to return her aunt's file this morning, and she desperately needed to get her hands on it. She couldn't hope to fool Slade indefinitely. The sooner she could get her hands on the information she needed the better.

Half the morning was gone before Drew appeared. Lisa was on the telephone when he walked in. She smiled a greeting, her eyes lighting up when she saw the folder in his hand.

It added a special glow to her smile that she was unaware of and caused Drew's quick intake of breath. While she transferred the phone call to Slade, Drew sat on the edge of her desk, gazing at her silently.

"It's a crime for someone so beautiful to be married," he declared when the transfer had been made.

"My husband doesn't think so," she smiled faintly, concealing her impatience to take the folder from his hand.

"Oh, yes," Drew nodded ruefully, then frowned. "What's his name again?" Lisa drew a complete blank. She couldn't remember the name she had given her fictitious husband. "Burt, that's it." Fortunately he supplied it. "Lucky Burt."

"Yes." But Lisa wanted to get off that subject before she buried herself in lies. "I see you brought the folder back safely."

"Yup, it's all here intact," he assured her, depositing it on the desk top. Lisa's fingers inched to open it and peruse the contents. It was an almost uncontrollable urge that she checked with a great deal of effort. "What about lunch today?"

"I'll have to take a raincheck," she refused, knowing

exactly how she intended to spend her lunch hour—glued to the folder.

"Come on, have a heart," Drew coaxed. "Make a poor bachelor happy for an hour."

"Sorry." Her mind wasn't going to be changed by any amount of flattery. "I'm behind with a lot of correspondence. I'm going to do what you did yesterday—have Ellen bring me back a sandwich to eat here."

"Okay," he capitulated unexpectedly. "If that's what you want, I'll buy the sandwich and we'll have a little picnic right here in the office."

"No," Lisa protested instantly, then tried to temper the sharpness of her refusal. "If you join me, then we'll talk and I won't get anything done, which would defeat my purpose for not going out to lunch. Let's just make it another day."

"I suppose I'll have to console myself with the knowledge that you didn't turn me down flat." Drew gave an exaggerated sigh.

"Exactly," she laughed briefly. "Now run off so I can get some work done." Her hands inched toward the folder as he straightened from her desk.

"You're a worse slave driver than Slade," he joked. "But a beautiful one."

With a wink and a wave of his hand, he left, and Lisa's hands greedily snatched up the folder, flipping it open to briefly scan the contents. The very first document caught her attention. It seemed to be a power of attorney.

Before she had a chance to examine it, there was the alerting sound of a doorknob being turned. She barely had time to close the folder when Slade walked in, aloof curiosity in his dark eyes at her guilty start.

"Is something wrong, Mrs. Eldridge?" His hard, handsome mouth softened slightly as if bemused by her reaction.

"No, I—I just didn't hear you, that's all." Her fingers tightened nervously on the stiff cover of the folder.

His dark gaze slid to the folder. "What do you have there?"

"Oh, er, this?" Damn, Lisa thought, she had to stop stammering like an errant child. "It's the Talmadge file. Drew just returned it, and I was just going to put it back in the cabinet."

"There's no need." He held out his hand. "I'll take it. There's a couple things in there I want to look over."

No, she cried inwardly, her fingers tightening convulsively on the folder. Aloud she murmured a hopeful, "Now?"

"Of course now." There was a humorless, silent laugh in his voice.

It had been a ridiculous question. Grudgingly Lisa handed it to him, unable to argue her right to keep it. "Was there anything else?" she asked, reverting to a taut, professional tone.

"No, nothing else." His gaze narrowed briefly on her before he shifted his attention to the folder in hand reentered his office.

Twice the file had been in her grasp and twice it had been taken from her. Frustration was beginning to set in.

Her assertion to Drew that she was going to have lunch at her desk trapped Lisa into spending the noon hour in her office. Although Slade had taken her aunt's file, she was determined all this time wasn't going to be wasted. Perhaps she could find some incriminating evidence in the files of the decorators, carpenters, and landscape company Slade used.

The trouble was that she didn't know their names and she wasn't any nearer to understanding the filing system. Her own code of ethics wouldn't permit her to examine a file unless something in its title had reference to the type of firm she was seeking. This seemed to eliminate the bulk of the folders.

Before the lunch hour was over, Lisa knew how a spy felt. Every creaking floorboard in the old building made her jump. Voices filtering in from the street had her looking around in alarm. Snooping was an unpleasant occupation, especially when one came up with zero results.

The sound of Slade's voice in the outer reception area sent her scurrying to her desk. She was bent over the paper in her typewriter when he walked into her office. Lisa pretended an absorption in her work rather than look up.

"Have there been any calls for me?" He stopped at her desk.

"No, sir." She made an unnecessary erasure of a word she had typed much earlier and blew the erasure dust from the paper.

"I'm expecting Clyde Sanders to stop by. When he arrives, send him into my office," Slade instructed.

"Yes, sir." Lisa nodded her compliance and sighed with relief when he walked into his private office and closed the door.

CHAPTER FIVE

BY THE END of the day, Lisa was engulfed in frustration. She had kept waiting and waiting for Slade to return her aunt's folder so that it could be filed... after, of course, she had looked through it. But he hadn't.

Shortly after three that afternoon, Slade had left the office on an errand. Desperate, Lisa had sneaked into his office to see if he had left the folder behind. She couldn't find it among the papers on his desk. One drawer of his desk had been locked and he had taken his briefcase with him. Lisa had presumed it was in one of the two places.

This deception was threatening to last much longer than she had ever intended. The longer it continued, the greater became the risk of being unmasked. Lisa knew she had to take advantage of every opportunity. If an opportunity didn't present itself, she would have to try to arrange one.

A few minutes after five, Lisa was still at the typewriter. Her plan was to keep working until after Slade had left and hopefully find the folder in the briefcase he had brought back with him. Slade was in his office with a client. No matter how tired she was or how much her body ached, Lisa was determined to outwait him.

Her patience was rewarded five minutes later when

she heard the connecting door open to Slade's private office and the voices of the two men talking as they came out. Her fingers continued tapping at the typewriter keys.

Lisa faked a concentration in her task and hoped Slade would leave with the man. But he walked with him only as far as the door to the reception area and bid him goodbye. When the client was gone, Slade turned. Lisa felt his gaze rest on her. Her skin prickled with her awareness of it, sensitive nerve ends reacting. But she tried to give no sign that she knew he was looking at her.

"It's after five, Mrs. Eldridge," he spoke, not allowing Lisa to ignore him any longer. "You should have left twenty minutes ago."

Her fingers paused on the keys as she gave him a preoccupied glance. "I'll be leaving shortly," she assured him with vague indifference.

"You do realize your children will be home from school by now."

His statement paralyzed Lisa. He said it as if she had children. Among all the lies she'd told, had she claimed to have children? She searched her memory. Unless it had failed her, Lisa was positive that she hadn't.

"I don't have any children, Mr. Blackwell," she corrected that impression. "My husband and I have decided to wait a few years before beginning a family."

"Regardless, your husband will be home expecting his dinner."

Lisa seethed at that typically male statement, but as Ann Eldridge, she didn't dare voice her feminist views on the subject of equality of sexes, nor her opinion that a husband could start dinner if his wife worked late. So she had to find another plausible reason why it wasn't essential for her to be home immediately.

"Undoubtedly my husband is working late, too," she said.

"Oh? What does he do?" Slade asked.

"He's in construction. When the weather is as beautiful as it is today, he gets in a lot of overtime. I'll be home before he is, even if I stay until six." Lisa shrugged her unconcern.

"There isn't any need for you to stay late."

"I want to finish this. You can go ahead and leave." *The sooner, the better,* Lisa added to herself. "As soon as I'm through here, I'll be going home, too, but I know how important it is—" ·

"Nothing is so important that it can't wait until tomorrow," Slade interrupted. "Your attitude is very commendable, Mrs. Eldridge, but unnecessary."

"But I don't mind staying," Lisa protested.

A dark eyebrow lifted at her persistence. "I said it wasn't necessary. Cover your typewriter and clear your desk. This is an order, Mrs. Eldridge," he stated.

"Very well." Lisa should have been grateful for his thoughtful consideration, but he had thwarted her attempt to stay late. She was frustrated once again.

Slade stood by her desk for several more seconds. Lisa shook out the plastic cover for the typewriter and draped it over the machine. The action apparently satisfied him that she intended to comply with his order and he returned to his private office.

Lisa took her time clearing the desk and putting things away. She used every excuse to linger, sharpening pencils and arranging the articles on her desk in a precise order. There was still a chance Slade might leave before she did. Ten minutes later, she was straightening a stack of papers in her file tray as Slade walked out of his office.

His gaze narrowed on her sharply, his features lean and hard. "Are you still here, Mrs. Eldridge? I thought I told you to go home."

"I was just straightening my desk." She took the blank stationery paper from beside the typewriter and returned it to its proper desk drawer. "I'll be leaving in a few minutes."

His mouth thinned as he turned and walked to the file cabinet. The hope that he might be on his way home, died as he removed two folders and returned to his office. There was nothing Lisa could do but leave and hope for better luck the next day.

Walking the blocks to her aunt's house, Lisa tried to formulate some plan of action, but she was too tired and vaguely dispirited to think. The wig in her purse seemed to weigh a ton. She had barely entered the house, the door not yet closed, when Mitzi's questioning voice sought her out.

"Lisa, is that you?" She came sweeping out of the living room into the foyer. "Gracious, I was about to send out a search party for you."

"I'm sorry I'm late," Lisa apologized, a faint, tired sigh in her voice. "I didn't mean for you to worry."

"You look exhausted. Sightseeing all day must have worn you out." A sympathetic smile curved her aunt's mouth. "Did you try to see everything in one day?"

"Something like that," she hedged and arched her

back to ease her cramped and sore muscles. "Right now the only thing I want to see is a tubful of hot water."

"A nice hot bath works wonders. You go soak for a while," Mitzi instructed. "Later you can come downstairs and join me in a relaxing drink before dinner."

"I'll do that," Lisa agreed and climbed the spiral staircase to her room.

While the bathtub was filling with water, Lisa undressed. Halfway to the bathroom she remembered the wig was still crammed in her purse. She took it out and hid it in the rear of a dresser drawer. She followed the scent of the fragrant bubble bath to the tub, turned off the faucets and climbed in. Lisa had no idea how long she lay soaking in the bath, but the water was cool when she climbed out to towel herself dry.

Lisa sighed dispiritedly as she slipped on the silk kimono-styled dressing robe that was chocolate brown and embroidered in pale ivory. The long bubble bath had eased the stiffness of her muscles, but it had done little to wash away the troubled light in her green eyes. Each day spent as Ann Eldridge was a risk.

Opening her closet door, she immediately turned away. She didn't feel like dressing even though she knew Mitzi was waiting downstairs for her to join her. The silk robe swished softly about her ankles as she walked barefoot to her bedroom door.

Maybe her aunt wouldn't stand on ceremony. A quiet evening spent lounging around was what Lisa dearly wanted and needed. She seriously doubted if Mitzi would object.

Her hand reached for the carved banister of the

staircase. Something—a sound, a voice—stopped her, her foot poised on the edge of the first step. At the bottom of the stairs stood Slade Blackwell, dark, arresting and vital. The sight of him paralyzed Lisa, and her hand clutched the loose fold of her robe together at the waist.

Insolently, his gaze slowly traveled the length of her. She reddened as she realized her action had drawn the clinging fabric more tightly over her curves, possibly revealing that she wore nothing beneath it.

Her skin seemed to burn from the appraising caress of his eyes, mocking yet suggestive. She released the robe immediately, spreading her fingers to try to relieve the sudden, elemental tension that claimed her.

"What are you doing here?" She finally broke the silence, her voice ringing with a challenge born of embarrassment.

"I don't think it's any of your business since I'm here to see Mitzi," he replied smoothly.

"Why?"

"I told you, it's none of your business." Slade continued to study her feminine shape with an arrogant unconcern that had to have been bred into him. The almost physical touch of his gaze was having disturbing effect on her senses, but Lisa was determined not to reveal it. Being dressed—or barely dressed—as she was, was enough of a disadvantage.

"Mitzi is my aunt and that makes your presence here my business," she retorted.

"The lawyer-client relationship doesn't recognize your right." His mouth twisted cynically. "*If* you have one."

"Where's Mitzi?" Lisa demanded.

"She misplaced her glasses and is off looking for them." He caught her gaze and held it. "Why don't you come down and entertain me?"

"I'm not dr—" The word "dressed" died on her lips. She was not usually so slow on the uptake. The entertainment he had meant didn't require clothes, as his throaty chuckle mockingly told her. "You're disgusting," she hissed.

But Slade appeared to ignore her insulting comment. His dark head was tipped slightly to the side, studying her with a seemingly new-found interest, puzzled and curious.

"There's something different about you," he drawled thoughtfully. "Maybe it's in your eyes, minus their sunglasses."

Lisa stiffened. He couldn't see the color of her eyes at this distance, not with the length of the staircase separating them. But his remark acted like a cold splash of ice water.

"There's nothing different about you!" she flashed defensively. "Tell Mitzi I'll be down when you leave."

Pivoting on her heel, she hurriedly retraced the way to her bedroom, trembling with delayed shock. That had been close, much too close.

Slade's appearance changed Lisa's mind about lounging around the house in her robe. In her room, she slipped out of the robe and put on a pair of pale yellow slacks and a blouse of a green and yellow print. She waited until she heard the front door close before venturing downstairs again. Mitzi was alone in the living room when Lisa entered it.

"You look better. How do you feel?" Mitzi walked to the wooden trolley cart and fixed Lisa a drink.

"Much better." Especially now that Slade was gone. Lisa settled into the orange- and rust-colored brocade chair. Slade's refusal to say why he had wanted to see Mitzi prompted Lisa to ask, "What did Slade want?" She didn't mention that she had spoken to him.

"He stopped over with some legal papers that needed my signature," her aunt explained.

"Oh?" Lisa took the drink her aunt brought her and sipped at it, wishing she had gotten a glimpse at those papers. "What kind of document was it? You did it read it before you signed it, didn't you?" she questioned, suddenly wary.

"I read it, but all that legal jargon is just so much mishmash. Who can understand it? If I wrote my novels like that, the readers would never be able to figure out the plot," Mitzi laughed with absolute unconcern.

"Do you mean that you don't know what you signed?" Lisa accused in astonishment.

"Slade explained it all to me," came the smooth assurance, which didn't reassure Lisa at all. Mitzi lowered her voice to a conspiratorial whisper. "I'm setting up a retirement fund for Mildred. Nothing very large, mind you, but something that will supplement her government pension when she reaches old age. She has been so loyal to me, and a friend, as well, despite her crabbiness. She's a regular skinflint, but I know she hasn't been able to put very much aside. This retirement program seemed a good way to help her without making it look like charity. Slade agreed when I mentioned it to him."

"I see." It sounded harmless. Lisa hoped it was.

Mitzi leaned back in her chair. "Tell me, what all did you see today?"

Lisa dreaded having to come up with more lies. She took a deep breath and tried to come up with a story that wouldn't trip her up.

"After breakfast, we took a carriage ride." Since that was one thing she had promised herself she would do. "The driver took us all around. As a matter of fact, we came right by here."

"I wish you had stopped for coffee. I would like to have met your friends. You are welcome to have them over anytime," Mitzi said.

"I thought about bringing them in," she lied, "but I knew you were busy with your new novel. By the way, how is it coming along?"

"Marvelously." Her aunt's face seemed to light up with excitement. "I'm getting to what I call the 'good' part. It's where the plot begins to thicken, if you'll pardon the use of a cliche." She began explaining the twists and turns of the plot, the element of suspense that was beginning to build, and the characters.

The rest of the evening Lisa adroitly maneuvered the conversation to focus on Mitzi's interests and avoided telling more lies about places she had supposedly seen. That night in bed, she questioned how much longer she was going to be able to get away with this deception. It seemed that only time would tell.

LISA LEANED OVER her typewriter when Slade walked out of his private office, pretending to read over the partially typed letter. He paused briefly beside her desk.

"I'm going to lunch now, Mrs. Eldridge. I'll be back shortly after one," he informed her.

After her near unmasking last night, Lisa took pains to avoid looking directly at him just in case some expression or gesture struck a familiar note. Even now when he was addressing her directly, she kept her head turned down, feigning a concentration in her work.

"Yes, Mr. Blackwell," she replied in a deliberately absent manner.

When he walked away, her green eyes followed him through the concealing veil of her sooty lashes. His day's calendar of appointments had indicated a business luncheon, but he wasn't carrying his briefcase. She breathed in deeply, knowing it meant it was still in his office.

From the reception area, she could hear him speaking to Drew. Hurriedly she began typing, removing the finished letter from the typewriter just as she heard the street door open and close. Slade was gone.

Lisa quickly separated the carbon copy of the letter from the original and set it aside. Taking the original and gathering up the other correspondence ready for his signature, she darted into his office.

The expensively tooled briefcase was on the floor behind the large swivel chair at his desk. Lisa shoved the papers on top of his desk and bent to open the briefcase. Her hands shook badly as she unsnapped the latch.

She felt like a thief and had to remind herself that Slade was the real thief. Still, her hearing was acutely tuned to any sound of invasion from the outer office.

Her aunt's file was not in the briefcase. Lisa rose in

irritation, looking at the endless stacks of papers and folders on his desk. She began riffling through them, searching for her particular needle in the haystack of papers.

"What are you doing, Mrs. Eldridge?" Slade's cold voice demanded.

Lisa froze for a panicked second, staring in disbelief that he could have approached so soundlessly. There was a ruthlessly hard look to his black eyes that made her toes curl.

Nervously she moistened her lips and tried to smile. "I brought some letters in for your signature." But that didn't explain what she was doing going through the other papers and his silence reminded her of it. "Your desk was in such a mess, I thought I'd straighten it."

"Thank you." Polite words without any sincerity. "But I prefer the mess," he stated icily. "Strange as it may seem to you, I know where everything is."

"I'm sorry." Lisa backed away from the desk, self-consciously aware of her foot bumping against his briefcase. A few moments earlier and she would have had a great deal more to explain. "I only meant to be helpful."

"In the future, confine your help to the outer office," Slade replied crisply, but apparently accepting her explanation. "Would you hand me my briefcase?"

"Of course." To give it to him, Lisa had to walk around the desk, her nerves leaping in awareness.

"It's nearly noon. Since you have the letters done, you might as well take your lunch break now." With case in hand, Slade courteously stepped to the side to let her precede him.

"I will," she agreed.

Any hope of going through his office at noon vanished as he waited expectantly in her outer office. Haphazardly she tidied her desk, gathered her hand-bag and spring jacket and led the way out of the building. In the street, they parted company with Slade issuing only a curt nod.

Lisa worked late, but Slade worked later. It was after six when she dashed into Mitzi's house. Her aunt was nowhere in sight, and Lisa was given a reprieve from explaining where she had been all day.

She had less than an hour to get ready before Slade arrived to take her and Mitzi to dinner. After undress-ing and bathing in record time, she reapplied her makeup and hurried to the closet.

Her choice of clothes was limited to the blue dress she had worn before and a satiny pantsuit in an unusual champagne shade, very nearly the color of her pale blond hair. A touch of vanity made her pick the pantsuit rather than wear something Slade had already seen. Lastly, she set the smoke blue sunglasses on the bridge of her nose, disguising the jewel green of her eyes.

At ten past seven, she hurried from her room to find Slade waiting at the bottom of the stairs. "I'm sorry I'm late." There was a hint of breathlessness in her voice—due entirely to the haste in getting ready, she was certain.

"That's quite all right." His hand took possession of her elbow, not letting her slacken her pace. "My car is outside." As he reached around her to open the door, his dark gaze skimmed her face. Her eyes were securely masked from his inspection by the sunglasses perched on her nose. "I see you're back to the sunglasses again."

"I did too much sight-seeing today." The story she had rehearsed for Mitzi sprang immediately to her lips.

"You seem to have a tendency to overdo things," Slade commented dryly.

You can say that again, Lisa thought. What had begun as innocent concern for her aunt had turned into a full-scale spying operation. It would be humorous if she wasn't so deeply ensnared in her own trap. But never in her life had she been half way involved in anything. It was always all or nothing.

The fragrant blossoms of the azaleas scented the dusk, their vibrant colors muted by the waning light. The bearded oaks cast dark shadows on the Lincoln Mark V parked in the driveway parallel to the portico entrance.

"I'll sit in the back. Mitzi can have the front seat," Lisa volunteered as Slade stepped ahead of her to open the car door. She intended to be a mouse in the corner that evening, observing, saying as little as possible.

"It's too late," he announced, more or less propeling her into the empty front seat and closing the door.

Turning in the plushy molded seat covered in a rich, midnight-blue velour, Lisa said, "Mitzi, I—" There was no one in the back seat. "Where's Mitzi?" she demanded of Slade as he slid behind the wheel.

"She's not coming." The key was in the ignition and being turned.

"What?" Stunned, Lisa stared at his boldly defined profile. "Why not?"

"Something to do with her heroine being in danger and she couldn't leave her novel until the hero had managed to rescue the girl." He shifted the car into gear, not sparing a glance in Lisa's direction.

"You put Mitzi up to this!" she accused in an angry hiss.

"I know you think I have unlimited power over Mitzi—" the look he flicked to her glinted with mockery "—but contrary to your belief, I have no control over the machinations of her writing. Nothing short of the end of the world could have dragged Mitzi away from the typewriter tonight."

"And I'm supposed to believe that?"

"I don't particularly care," he said with an expressively indifferent lift of his shoulder.

"Well, I'm certainly not going out alone with you!" Then Lisa realized the car was moving, its powerful motor purring almost silently as they glided through the narrow streets. They were easily two blocks from Mitzi's house. "You can turn this car right around and take me back," she ordered stiffly.

"No."

She grabbed at the door handle, but it wouldn't budge. "Unlock this door!"

"No."

Lisa was furious. She fumbled along the armrest, seeking the power lock control for her door. The seat moved with one switch; the window rolled down with another before she heard the click of the door.

As she reached for the handle, her arm was caught in a vice. She tried to twist away from the grip and it slid along the satin-smooth material of her long sleeve

Then her hand was swallowed in the engulfing hold of his.

"Let me go!"

"You could at least wait until I've stopped the car," Slade taunted. "Or are you intent on breaking your neck?"

"Then stop it!" She was rigidly aware of the strength of his large hand. With the slightest pressure, he could break the slender bones in her hand and fingers, yet there was no pain.

"I can't stop here, I have a car behind me. You'll have to wait until I can pull over," he reasoned with irritating calm.

The street didn't widen until they turned onto Battery. Slade kept a firm hold of her hand until he had parked the car next to the curb. The instant he released her Lisa was out of the car in a flash, only to hear the motor switched off and his car door slam.

She darted into White Point Garden, hoping to lose herself in the dark shadows under the trees, but the pale, shiny material of her pantsuit was like a beacon in the darkness. He was at her side within seconds, capturing her wrist to slow her down.

She spun around. "I thought I'd make it plain that I don't want your company. I wouldn't go to heaven with you!"

"You're overdoing the dramatics, Lisa." His tone was dry with indulgence.

"If I am, it's because you drive me to it," she snapped. "You know very well that the only reason I agreed to this dinner tonight was because of Mitzi. That's why you manhandled me into the car and drove off without warning me in advance that she'd begged off. Whatever made you think I would agree to go out alone with an embezzler like you?"

"To talk."

"About what? What a low, despicable character I think you are?" Lisa strained against his hold on her wrist, trembling with the ferocity of her anger.

"I have a red-haired secretary who is better tempered than you are," Slade laughed. It was a low mocking sound.

For a split second, alarm kept her silent. "Take her out to dinner, then. I'm sure it really doesn't matter to you that she's married. All that regret about her ineligibility was just for Mitzi's benefit."

"You see right through me, don't you?" His remark was riddled with amusement.

"Yes, and I don't like what I see."

"That's a pity, because I like what I see." He loomed closer, his dark head shadowing her face.

Lisa retreated instinctively, remembering his avenging kiss in the study. He followed as she continued to back up warily until her shoulders were pressed against the rough bark of a tree trunk. Her breath was coming unevenly, yet she wasn't exactly afraid.

There were others wandering in the park, and not even Slade Blackwell would accost her in a public place. Not releasing her wrist, he brought his other arm up to lean a hand against the trunk near her head.

His nearness was having its effect on her senses, though. The musky fragrance of his shaving lotion was an erotic stimulant, wafting near her face in an enveloping cloud. There was a latent sensuality to his disturbing masculinity. His near-black eyes were lazily focused on her lips, moistened in nervousness. Lisa was left in little doubt as to what direction his interest was taking. Her pulse refused to behave normally, skipping beats when she needed most to remain calm.

"I've had time to think about our conversation—or should I call it confrontation—the other night." There was a decidedly caressing tone to his low voice. His thumb slid beneath the cuff of her sleeve to the inside of her wrist, rubbing her pulse point with disturbing results.

"What about it?" Lisa had to swallow the breathless catch in her voice.

"I've decided that it's mutually defeating to declare war on each other."

The lazy softening of his hard mouth into a smile was a bit too potent in its charm for Lisa to handle. She looked beyond him to the dark mound of a cannon, a relic of the Civil War permanently mounted in the garden. Its barrel pointed across the bay waters to the distant fortress of Fort Sumter.

"What are you suggesting?" *There*, Lisa sighed inwardly. She sounded much more in control of herself when she issued that question.

"That we effect a compromise."

"What kind?" The smoke blue lenses of her glasses shaded the green of her eyes, but they didn't lessen the sharpness of the look she darted at Slade.

"The kind that lets us join forces."

"Impossible!"

"Why is it impossible?" Slade argued smoothly.

"Why should we keep fighting one another? We'd both end up losing."

He still believed she was intervening because she wanted Mitzi's money. That was what he wanted, and he obviously believed it was the only thing she was interested in. Lisa hesitated. Perhaps this was another way of gaining the proof against him that she needed.

Slade noticed her hesitation and pressed his advantage. "It makes sense, doesn't it?"

"Perhaps," Lisa conceded, at least temporarily until she could think his suggestion through. She moved her wrist slightly against his hold. "Please, I'd like to walk." What she really needed was to get some distance between them so she could think clearly.

Obligingly Slade released her wrist and fell in step beside her when she pushed away from the tree trunk. But she didn't obtain the complete separation she desired. Vaguely possessive, his hand rested on the lower curve of her spine. The smooth material made his touch seem all the more sensuous against her skin.

She was much too aware of the man at her side, aware of him as a man. She had to remind herself of the character of the man beneath the tall, muscular physique. If she had needed any confirmation, she had received it a moment ago when he had suggested they work together to obtain Mitzi's money. She almost had to agree to go along with him so she could prove to Mitzi what Slade Blackwell really was.

Her attention shifted to the body of water glistening ahead of her in the twilight. The White Point Garden was located virtually on the tip of the peninsula of Old Charleston. Lisa's steps faltered, slowing almost to a stop as she stared at the water.

The surface was smooth and reflecting, giving no indication of the current flowing underneath. It reminded her of Slade. She had no idea what was going on inside his mind.

"The Ashley River," Slade quietly identified the body of water. "This is where the Ashley and the Cooper rivers flow together to form the Atlantic Ocean," he explained, voicing the whimsical tongue-in-cheek claim of the Charlestonians.

"I'm not interested in a geography lesson," Lisa returned impatiently. She turned to face him, tipping her head back slightly to see his features. "How do I know I can trust you?"

"How do *I* know I can trust you?" he countered.

"That's not an answer."

"The answer is we would have to trust each other."

"Honor among thieves and all that?" Lisa taunted sarcastically. "You don't know the meaning of the word honor."

"Do you?"

"I am not Mitzi's attorney bound by law to protect her interests," she reminded him.

"No, you're Mitzi's niece. Shall we begin comparing the blackness of the pot and the kettle?" Slade challenged dryly.

Her lips tightened grimly as she looked away. "You can't honestly expect me to forget your crude behavior the other night. No," she shook her head in agitation, "it would never work."

"You were the one who started the hostilities, Lisa."

"Because I slapped your face?"

"Didn't your mother ever teach you that you could win more friends with flattery? Or wasn't I supposed to catch the veiled insults you threw at me all that evening?"

"That was not an excuse for you to manhandle me," she snapped.

He was calmly and deliberately baiting her and, fool that she was, she was rising to snap at it. She breathed in deeply. She would not let him make her lose her temper.

"No, it wasn't an excuse, but—" Slade paused for effect "—it was only a kiss."

"Is that what you call it?" The retort was out before she could stop it.

"Issued in a moment of anger, I'll admit," he answered, revealing only amusement at her gibe.

"To put it mildly," Lisa snapped.

"You provoked that anger, to put it mildly," Slade mocked her.

"If that's the way you feel, why this sudden change?"

"With each of us tearing at Mitzi trying to convince her the other is no good, no matter which way it goes, we're going to end up putting doubt in her mind about each of us," he reasoned.

"And a third party could end up with all the money." Lisa followed the thought to its logical conclusion.

"Unless we come to an agreement," he added.

"Very well, tell me more about this agreement you want me to make," she breathed in decision.

"We'll discuss it after dinner." Slade smiled, the pressure increasing on the back of her waist as he turned toward the car. "I booked a table for seven-thirty. We're late, but I'm sure they'll hold our reservations for us. In the meantime, let's call a truce."

"A truce?" Lisa laughed in disbelief. "Are you serious?"

"Naturally I'm serious," he said, guiding her past a tall magnolia. "You need time to get used to the idea of trusting me."

"I doubt if I ever will," Lisa said, and meant it.

"You've made progress," he commented.

"Why?"

"Because you said 'doubt,' before you simply made it a flat statement that you never would." A glitter of arrogant complacency was in his look.

"A technicality," she dismissed the argument.

"Remember?" A dark brow arched in wry amusement. "My profession deals in technicalities."

"I'm afraid you're indulging in a bit of wishful thinking," Lisa denied a bit more sharply than she had intended.

Slade glanced at her as he reached to open the passenger door of the car. He didn't say anything, just let a faint smile touch the edge of his mouth.

CHAPTER SIX

CONTENTED, LISA DECIDED—that was the only word to describe the way she felt. The restaurant was sumptuously elegant yet relaxing at the same time, two qualities that did not necessarily go hand in hand.

The food had been excellent and her head was a bit fuzzy from the wine, but it was a pleasurable kind of fuzziness. She took another sip of the dry white wine in the stemmed glass. Soft music played in the background, gently romantic, setting the mood.

The table was small, intimately so with Slade sitting directly across from her. Lisa studied him openly, the intensity of her green gaze masked by the tinted lenses of her glasses. His roguishly thick mane of hair had a raven sheen to it, his eyes like black diamonds glittered with an inner fire.

His tanned features could have been chiseled in stone, yet they were so very male and so very compelling. Stone was wrong; no stone could ever possess the vitality that Slade had.

That vitality and charm had been working its magic on Lisa all evening. Slade's particular brand of charm was more potent than others she had known because it was so subtle. He didn't use an ounce of flattery, yet he made Lisa feel so good inside. It made him dangerous, but at the moment she was in the mood to flirt with danger.

It was crazy the way her mind was capable of dividing itself. One part of it was thinking about him, analyzing the things about him that set him apart from ordinary men. Another part was registering every word he said so she could make the appropriate responses when they were required.

The third part of her mind was noting other things about him. She liked the low pitch of his voice, smooth and rich like velvet. And she liked the way the corners of his mouth deepened when he thought something was amusing but didn't openly smile.

He said something dryly funny and Lisa laughed. "I was beginning to think you'd drifted away somewhere. You should laugh like that more often." A slow smile spread across his mouth, making an impact on her pulse.

"And you should smile like that more often," she returned, aware of the husky tremor in her voice, but not caring.

"We're beginning to sound like a mutual admiration society," Slade pointed out dryly, amused and mocking.

"Mitzi would be astounded," Lisa declared laughingly.

"I doubt it. Knowing Mitzi and her penchant for happy endings, she would find a romantically logical reason." Instantly something flashed across his face—a look of irritation or impatience, but Lisa couldn't be sure which. "Mildred mentioned that you'd barely returned to the house when I arrived. You were out sight-seeing with your friends?" The subject was deftly changed.

Lisa wondered why. Surely Slade didn't think she was becoming romantically attracted to him. Well, wasn't she, a small voice jeered. Wasn't she just a little bit curious what it would be like if he made love to her? She was afraid any answer she gave would be self-incriminating and she tried to ignore the questions.

"I was out with Peg and Susan for part of the day," she lied. "I browsed through the shops in the morning and the three of us went sightseeing in the afternoon."

"Where did you go?"

She hesitated for only a fraction of a second before she remembered a brochure she had seen. "Brookgreen Gardens. The statuary there is breathtaking. Unfortunately we got caught in the rush-hour traffic on the way back—that's why I was so late."

"There are some very fine American sculptors represented there," Slade agreed. "Which was your favorite?"

Was he testing her? Lisa wondered, then decided not. "They were all so beautiful it's impossible to pick one," she hedged.

"True. Brookgreen Gardens is very impressive, especially with its avenue of live oaks."

"Yes, isn't it?" Lisa smiled.

"Shall we go?" Slade asked unexpectedly. "I believe the restaurant is closing."

"What?" Lisa glanced around, surprised to see only two other tables occupied in the dining room. "Yes, of course."

As she reached for her handbag, Slade moved to the back of her chair. "It was a delicious meal. Thank you," she offered, rising as he held the chair out.

"My pleasure." But there was something distant in his reply.

The car was parked nearly a block away. Slade insisted that Lisa wait outside the restaurant for him to bring it around. As his long, smooth strides carried him away, she shivered slightly, feeling she had been abandoned to the cool of the evening.

Flames from the torches mounted on the building front flickered over the brick walls and the boarded, arched windows. Lisa shifted nearer to their light just as the sleek Lincoln drove up to the curb in front of the restaurant.

There was no indication of the chilling aloofness she thought she had detected in Slade moments earlier. She decided it must have been her imagination that made her think he had suddenly withdrawn. There was nothing cool about his attitude as he helped her into the passenger seat. In fact, his smile was quite disarming when he turned to her after sliding behind the wheel.

"Would you like to go directly back to Mitzi's or do you want to take a driving tour of Old Charleston by night?" Slade asked.

It was late and she would have to be up early to get to the office. The wisest choice would be to go directly to Mitzi's, but she heard her voice opting for the second choice.

"The driving tour."

She was crazy, she thought, settling back in her seat and smiling at herself. She disliked Slade yet she was dangerously attracted to him. She should feel wary instead of so contented.

"Why the smile?" He slowed the car as it turned a corner on to a rough, cobblestoned street.

"It must be the afterglow of good wine," Lisa sighed, confused by the change without really caring.

"I noticed it mellowed your temper."

"Yours, too," she countered, and glanced out the window.

The street they were on ran along the waterfront. On the opposite side of the docks were brightly painted old houses abutting each other. "How odd! Look." She pointed them out to Slade. "Each one is painted a different color."

He sent her a curious look. "That's Rainbow Row. I thought you'd been touring Charleston these past few days. How did you miss Rainbow Row?"

"Oh—" Lisa breathed in nervously, running the tip of her tongue over her lips "—I haven't toured Old Charleston yet. Mostly we've been taking other tours, like out to Fort Sumter and driving to the military academy."

"The Citadel?"

"Yes. I've been saving Old Charleston to see with Mitzi. She's used it and the Low Country of South Carolina so often as backdrops for her romances that I'm sure she would know all sorts of unique things about it. But tell me about Rainbow Row," she urged, wanting to get away from any detailed discussion about how she'd spent her time the past few days.

"The oldest house here dates from the 1740s. They're private residences, very much in demand. In the eighteenth century, this was the waterfront district. The different colors are a trademark, a means to set each one apart."

Passing the row of colorful houses, he turned at the corner. Lisa had the sensation of slipping into the past. With the buildings and houses shadowed by the night and few cars on the narrow streets, the modern touches seemed to be hidden from view, steeping the night in history.

Making another turn, Slade directed her attention to the house on the left. "The Heyward-Washington house, one of the places entitled to claim that 'George Washington slept here.' Thomas Heyward Jr. was one of the signers of the Declaration of Independence." Lisa had barely focused on the shadow-dimmed exterior when he pointed at something else. "Does that look familiar to you?"

"Vaguely," she admitted, wishing now the tour wasn't being made in the semidarkness. In the daylight she might recognize why it was familiar. Instead she had to ask. "Where have I seen it?"

"*Porgy and Bess,* the operetta. Cabbage Row inspired the setting for it. There used to be vegetable stands along the sidewalk, hence its name."

They drove down more streets, past more historic points of interest. It was a tour Lisa would have to make again by daylight. There was too much to see, but she was glad the first time had been by night. It had made the antique charm of the old section of the city come to life, its early glory more than just imagination.

She gazed silently out the window as Slade made another turn. She recognized the street, having walked it every day to his office. Her aunt's house was just off this street. Her gaze settled on a white mansion set back from the street, protected by lace grillwork and shadowed by massive guardian oaks, draped with Spanish Moss.

"Of all the mansions in Old Charleston, I think that one is the loveliest," she told Slade.

"Which one?"

"The one there," she pointed. "We're just approaching it."

"Would you like a closer look?" A half smile touched his mouth as he darted a questing look.

"Sure," Lisa agreed, thinking he meant that he would drive closer to the curb so she could have a better look at the mansion by night. Instead he turned the car in through the grillwork gates. "What are you doing?"

"You said you wanted a closer look," he mocked.

"Yes, but I didn't mean this close. Heavens, I walk by it every day—"

"You walk by it," his quiet voice immediately seized on her statement.

Lisa could have bit off her tongue. She blamed it on too much wine. She had been lulled into a false sense of security. She had to remember that Slade was still her adversary.

"Yes," she added with what had to be her millionth lie, "on my way to meet Susan and Peg. They usually pick me up at the corner." Even though his lean features were slightly shadowed, she could still see the twist of skepticism about his mouth. "We can't stop here," she protested as he stopped the car near the front entrance of the large white house.

"I know the owners very well," Slade insisted. "They won't mind if you have a look inside."

"There's no one home." The windows were dark, but it didn't bother Slade as he climbed out of the car and walked to Lisa's door.

"They're away, but they left the key with me," he explained, helping a confused and uncertain Lisa from the car.

"One of your clients?"

"More or less. I handle legal matters from time to time, but I've known them for years." His hand at her elbow guided her up the three steps to the door. Taking a key from his pocket, he inserted it in the lock and opened the door, switching on a light just inside the door before stepping back to let Lisa walk in first. "The house is closed up until fall, so the furniture has all been covered. But you can get an idea of the layout."

The oak floor of the foyer was polished to a high sheen. Ornate plaster cornices rimmed the ceiling. Light gleamed from the delicate crystal sconces on walls lined with paintings.

Still feeling like a trespasser, Lisa tentatively moved closer to inspect them. Her eyes widened at the first, a portrait of a man with raven hair and dark eyes, dressed in old-world clothes. Slade was just behind her and she pivoted to face him.

"The owners, they're relatives of yours," she accused.

"My parents," he smiled.

"Why didn't you tell me instead of letting me think that—" Lisa didn't voice the rest of her demanding question. She knew exactly how she would have ended it: something to the effect that the owners were more people he was systematically stealing from. For some reason she just didn't want to introduce that subject to their conversation. It was true, the wine had mellowed her somehow. It had taken the sharpness from her tongue and she didn't want to argue with him.

"Were you thinking the worst?" he mocked.

"Never mind. It doesn't matter." Lisa turned away, forcing the irritation she didn't understand from her voice. "Would you show me around?"

Despite the white sheets covering the furniture, there was a warmth to the house. Their footsteps echoed hollowly on the wood floors as they toured the rooms of the lower floor and followed the free-standing spiral staircase to the second. Yet the house didn't seem really empty.

"Don't your parents spend much time here?"

"Not any more—not since my father bought the farm," Slade admitted. "They spend all but the late autumn and early winter months there."

"He moved to the farm shortly after you joined the law practice, didn't he?" Lisa mused absently.

"Yes," Slade paused, his head tilting curiously. "How did you know?"

"Mitzi mentioned it to me, I guess." She shrugged, covering her slip with a lie. "Did you live here?"

"All my life." Slade started walking, his hand at her back drawing her with him.

"Why don't you live here now?" She looked at him curiously. "I mean," she laughed self-consciously, "it seems a shame for this beautiful old house to be empty for even a day."

"It's too big for one man."

"Yes, it's a family house," Lisa agreed, thinking of the numerous bedrooms meant for a brood of dark-haired, dark-eyed children. "Where do you live?"

"In the slave quarters behind the house," he told her. "We remodeled the building into a small bachelor apartment when I was in college. It's become quite popular to renovate the old quarters into apartments and rent them. Profitable, too."

"I suppose the next thing you'll do is invite me to your apartment. Every bachelor has a collection of etchings to show." Lisa said it in jest.

A roguish glint danced wickedly in his eyes. "Would you like to see my apartment?"

"Of course not." Her foot faltered on the stairstep. "It's just a standard bachelor line, isn't it?"

"So I've heard," Slade agreed. "But it's been so sadly overworked that no one uses it any more."

"That's good, because it's late, and I don't want Mitzi worrying about me. I'd better be getting back." *Before I end up in water over my head,* Lisa added silently. She was becoming much too friendly with Slade, the wrong kind of friendly. If she was going to be nice to him, it should be with the intention of getting information from him and not just to make small talk. He was making her lose sight of her goal.

"At least you have the advantage over me," Slade commented as they walked through the foyer to the front door. "You're on vacation and can sleep late in the morning. I have to be in the office first thing, which means getting up early."

"So do I." Lisa realized what she had said and rushed to cover it. "Not to be in the office, of course, but I'm meeting Peg and Susan first thing in the morning."

"Again? I thought you were here to visit Mitzi."

"I am, but she's in the middle of a book. It's silly for me to hang around the house every day waiting for her to finish. I might as well enjoy myself." She sounded more defensive than she wanted, but it couldn't be helped. "It is my vacation. Besides, I have the weekend to spend with Mitzi."

"Then you can act the dutiful and devoted niece, is that it?"

Her mouth opened to protest the tinge of sarcasm in his voice, but she caught herself in time. "I think I can play the role as effectively as you play yours as the loyal attorney."

The last light was switched off, throwing the mansion into darkness. Lisa waited at the steps while Slade locked the door. When he joined her, she started to descend the steps to the car, but his hand caught at her arm to stop her.

"I'm almost sorry the truce is over." He seemed to make the admission reluctantly.

Lisa agreed, but she wouldn't admit it. "You started it."

"You didn't waste any time making a retort."

"Did you expect me to turn the other cheek?"

"Would it have hurt you?" Slade countered.

His saturnine face was shadowed by the night darkness and Lisa couldn't see how much of his regret was mockery and how much of it was sincere.

"If you must know, yes, it would have," she returned sharply.

"We can't keep insulting each other if we're going to be partners."

"Who said we were going to be?" Lisa retorted. "I'm not convinced that I need you."

"Yes, you are. It just sticks in your craw to admit it." There was no mistaking the complacency in his tone. He was utterly sure of himself and Lisa.

"Maybe it's the other way around." She stubbornly resisted making the admission even though she knew she would eventually. Once Slade believed that she was on his side, he would confide exactly how he was obtaining Mitzi's money. "Maybe you need me more than I need you and you don't want to admit it."

"But I already have—when I made the proposal that we should work together," he reminded her. "What do you say? Are we partners?"

"I'd like to think about it." Now why did she say that? Lisa wondered. Did she want to make him sweat a little?

"What is there to think about? You know you've already made up your mind." He seemed to find her resistance amusing and futile.

"Maybe I have." Lisa tipped her head challengingly to one side, her silver blond hair shimmering in the faint light. "Maybe I've decided the answer is no. Did you think of that?"

He drew his head back, the angle faintly mocking, and she saw the corners of his mouth deepening. "If your answer was an outright no, you wouldn't have come with me tonight. You would have told me at the gardens to get lost. But you didn't. That means the answer is yes."

Lisa glanced away, her lips thinning. "You're very sure of yourself," she commented with irritation.

"No." His thumb and forefinger captured her chin and turned her back to face him. "I'm sure of you and the way your mind works."

His insolence was beyond belief, but it was the shiver of feeling evoked by his touch that claimed her. It rippled down her spine in tiny shock waves. Her throat was dry, incapable of speech.

Damn the wine, she thought. It was making her light-headed. The ground seemed unsteady beneath her feet, as if she was aboard a floating boat. Slade stood so tall and steady before her that she wanted to sway against his solidness and regain her equilibrium. It was the craziest sensation because she knew she was imagining all of it.

His gaze narrowed on her face, dark brows drawing together. His dark eyes seemed to physically touch each feature, inspecting, faintly caressing until they halted on her lips, softened in curious vulnerability. Slade bent his head toward her, then stopped as if waiting for a protest from Lisa.

There was a fevered awareness that he was going to kiss her and an equally shocking discovery that she wanted him to. This ambivalence toward him was insane, but she made not the slightest sound to stop him. His dark head began moving again, closing the distance until there was none.

The brush of his hard mouth against hers drew a tiny gasp, as her nerves tensed in shock. Lightly he explored the lips he had once plundered, sensually feeling his way. An eyebrow was quirked in puzzled surprise when he raised his head. Her lips were tingling with pleasure from his caressing kiss.

"It's crazy," she murmured, voicing the bewilderment she felt.

"Yes," Slade agreed, not needing to ask what she meant.

"I don't even like you," she added.

"I know."

His hand left her chin to spear his fingers through the spun silver of her hair at the back of her neck, tilting her head to meet his descending mouth. Her lips parted instinctively on contact, a golden storm of sensations racing through her body at his possession. There was nothing tentative in his kiss this time, and she felt the shuddering response she made to his demand.

Abruptly Slade drew away, frowning as he looked down at her. There was a hardness to the line of his jaw, a checked anger in his expression. Shaken by her reaction, Lisa turned away, trying to stop the leaping of her senses.

"We'd better leave," he said tightly.

"Yes," Lisa agreed fervently, wanting to conduct no more experiments in his embrace—if that was what she had been doing.

His hand was at her elbow, more or less propelling her down the short flight of steps to the car. He was still frowning when he helped her into the car and walked around to the driver's side. He reversed the car out of the driveway without saying a word. It was only a few minutes' drive to Mitzi's house, but the heavy silence made it seem much longer.

When he turned the car into the drive and stopped, Lisa didn't wait for him to get out of the car and walk her to the door, but darted out on her own. Her good-night was lost in the slam of her car door.

Slade didn't follow as she rushed to the door, nearly running as if there was something that frightened her. The only problem was that Lisa was afraid of herself. At her aunt's door, she glanced back at the car. Slade was watching her, a thoughtful frown still darkening his face.

As Lisa entered the house, her aunt walked out of the study. Lisa struggled to appear composed. Mitzi glanced at the watch on her wrist, her expression registering astonishment.

"Is it that late already?" she murmured.

Lisa immediately seized on the remark to keep the subject away from herself. "Have you been working all this time, Mitzi?"

"I guess I have." The admission was made with a faint laugh of surprise. "I became so involved with the manuscript that I lost track of the hour. I hope you didn't think I was waiting up for you."

"For a minute I did think I was living at home again with mom mysteriously appearing whenever I came home from a date," Lisa smiled nervously, remembering how astute her mother was at reading her mind. She hoped Mitzi didn't possess the same prowess.

"How was your evening? Did Slade take you some-place nice for dinner?" Mitzi asked.

"It was very nice." Which was a safe answer as Lisa sought to avoid more personal questions. There was a great deal of her own emotional reaction toward the evening that she had to sort out.

"I'm sorry I had to back out like that at the last minute." The apology was sincere. And Lisa was convinced that her aunt's excuse had been genuine and not an attempt to manipulate the evening so she and Slade would be forced to be together.

"Slade explained why you couldn't come. I hope you managed to rescue your heroine," Lisa offered.

"Oh, I did." Mitzi's emphatic nod was cut short by the onset of a yawn. "You must be as tired as I am. It's time we both were in bed."

"Yes, good night, Mitzi." She walked to the stairs, relieved that she had avoided any discussion of Slade.

"Good night, Lisa," her aunt returned and started down the hallway to her bedroom on the ground floor.

Upstairs in her room, Lisa changed into her night-clothes and crawled into bed. She didn't switch off the light right away as she stared at the swirling cream satin of the canopy. Everything seemed suddenly very complicated. It was because of that kiss and the way she had responded to it. But more and more, it was because of Slade. She turned off the light.

The next day it was difficult to face him as Ann Eldridge. Lisa tried to be indifferently professional around him and failed miserably. Fortunately Slade was too preoccupied to notice or he would have seen how nervous his temporary secretary was in his presence.

He was bending over her desk signing some correspondence she had typed and that he wanted in the mail that day. Lisa found herself studying the way the overhead light gave a blue black sheen to his hair.

Her gaze slid to his profile, to the hard male line of his mouth. Only last night, it hadn't been hard and unyielding when it covered hers. There had been a persuasive mastery to his kiss that her lips still remembered.

What was more important, she had let herself be persuaded to answer it. And it hadn't been an unpleasant experience. She only wished it had. It was so much easier to hate him than to be caught in conflicting reactions.

Her gaze shifted to the dark black of his eyes and found him returning her look with an absently puzzled quirk of his brow. Immediately, Liza glanced away, trying to cover the sudden confusion that brought a warmth to her cheeks.

"Is something wrong, Mrs. Eldridge?" he asked curiously.

"No, nothing," she rushed.

"Was there something you wanted to ask me?" Slade persisted.

"No. What could there be?" Lisa shrugged nervously.

"That's what I'm asking you."

Slade had been in a brooding mood all day. Because of that, this sudden interest in her made Lisa nervous and apprehensive. Perhaps he had noticed a resemblance between her and her other self. Lisa knew she had to be very careful.

"I assure you there's nothing." The letters were signed and she gathered them up to start folding them and putting them in their respective envelopes.

"If it's about your wages—"

"The agency pays me directly and will bill you later," she lied hurriedly. She wasn't going to accept his money when she was here to spy on him. "Was there anything else you wanted me to do?"

"Yes. Call Miriam Talmadge for me." Lisa paled at his clipped request. "Find out what time she expects her niece home this afternoon."

"Her niece?" Lisa repeated weakly, her face becoming even whiter.

"Yes, I believe that's what I said," he retorted impatiently.

"If—if Mrs. Talmadge should ask why you want to know, what should I tell her?" Her nerves were behaving as erratically as a jumping bean.

"Tell her it's none of her business." There was something savage in his snapped answer. Breathing in sharply, Slade immediately retracted his answer. "No, tell Mrs. Talmadge," he began, forcing himself to reply calmly to her question, "that I'll be over this evening to see Lisa—as well as Mrs. Talmadge," he added as a definite afterthought.

"All right," Lisa breathed, relieved that she was going to have advance warning of his visit.

Pushing back the tan sleeve of his suit jacket, Slade glanced at his gold watch. "If by some chance Mrs. Talmadge's niece should be there, put the call through to me and I'll talk to her. I'll be in Drew's office. If not, then pass the message on to me there as to when Mrs. Talmadge expects her back."

"I'll do that," Lisa promised, but Slade was already walking away, her compliance with his order anticipated.

After he had left her office, she toyed with the idea of speaking to him as Lisa Talmadge, pretending to be at her aunt's home. But there was too much risk that he might mention it to Mitzi, who would quickly deny that Lisa had been there.

Disguising her voice, she placed the call, informing Mildred of Slade's impending visit that evening, then crisply relayed the message to Slade that Lisa was expected home around six.

The knowledge that she would be seeing Slade that evening didn't make the day go faster. Instead it worked in the reverse, every minute dragging as she tried to guess his reason. Not knowing what to anticipate made her as skittish as a colt.

Her stomach was such a mass of knots that she was barely able to do justice to the meal Mildred had prepared. Every sound that came from outside of the house had her pulse skyrocketing, thinking it was Slade arriving.

"I don't know why Mildred didn't think to invite Slade to dinner," Mitzi sighed as she poured out the coffee and handed a cup to Lisa. "There was certainly enough food to go around, especially when you ate so little."

"I wasn't very hungry."

The cup was clattering in its saucer and Lisa realized that her hands were shaking. She quickly set the coffee on the table in front of the couch, clasping her hands together in her lap.

"I had a big lunch." The truth was she hadn't eaten anything. As as a result, she felt weak and trembling inside, but the thought of eating any of the small cakes on the coffee tray was repellent.

"You haven't told me how you and Slade got along last night." Mitzi settled back in her chair, her own coffee cup held steadily in her hands, a bright gleam in her brown eyes.

"Okay, I guess," Lisa tried to shrug away the question indifferently, but her aunt wasn't to be put off by her uninformative reply.

Clicking her tongue in mock reproof, Mitzi insisted, "Your answer is much too nonchalant, Lisa. It couldn't have been as bland an evening as that. Come now, what happened really?"

"I don't know what you mean," Lisa denied nervously. "We went out to eat. We talked, drove around a bit and he brought me home."

"No face-slapping? No fighting? Just a quiet little evening, is that it?" her aunt grinned knowingly.

"We argued, yes. Is that what you want me to say?" Lisa asked in agitation.

"But not all the time?"

Lisa rubbed her finger against the center of her forehead, trying to ease the throbbing pain. "No, not all the time," she admitted with a sigh.

"To be truthful, I didn't think you'd go out with him," her aunt commented.

"I didn't have much choice. He practically dragged me out of the house and into the car before I even found out you weren't coming along," she explained.

"That sounds like something Slade would do," Mitzi laughed to herself. "The two of you must have reconciled some of your differences after an evening together."

"I don't know." And that was the truth.

The doorbell rang and Lisa jumped. "That must be Slade," Mitzi announced unnecessarily.

As her aunt went to answer the door, Lisa rose from

the couch and walked to a window, lifting aside the curtain to stare outside. Without turning, she knew the instant Slade entered the room. She felt the touch of his gaze and tensed.

"Hello, Lisa." The greeting seemed to be forced from him, his tone clipped and taut.

"Hello, Slade." An artificial smile curved her mouth as she glanced over her shoulder.

The sharpness of his gaze seemed to thrust into her like a dagger, pinning her helplessly on its point. Relentlessly, he searched her expression, noting its strained tension. The vaguely angry frown was back on his face when he finally looked away. Released from his gaze, Lisa felt all the more confused about why he had come and why her heart was beating so wildly.

"We were just having coffee. You'll join us, won't you, Slade?" Mitzi invited, already reaching for the third cup sitting on the coffee tray.

"Yes." But the answer was given automatically without interest.

"You look troubled about something, Slade," Mitzi said, as she poured the coffee.

His dark gaze flicked to Lisa, ricocheting instantly away. "It was a rough day at the office. I guess I brought some of it with me."

That wasn't true. It had been one of the quietest days at the office, and Lisa wondered why he had lied about it. She stared at him, sensing his restlessness. Although he wasn't moving, she had the sensation of him prowling the room. It was as though they were on the same wavelength, except that Lisa didn't know the cause of his restlessness.

"Lisa, your coffee is getting cold," Mitzi reminded her.

"Sorry, I forgot." Then she wondered why she had apologized.

Her legs felt strangely weak as they carried her past Slade to the couch. She seemed to be caught up in his brooding mood, feeling the hidden disturbance as it grated on her nerve ends. His dark gaze was studying her, but she avoided meeting it.

Yet she was aware of his every move, of the coiled impatience in his controlled acceptance of the coffee cup. The muscles of her throat were beginning to constrict with the tension. She could only manage tiny sips of her lukewarm coffee.

"I didn't have an opportunity the other night to look at that review of your latest book, Mitzi," Slade said. "I'd like to read it."

"I'll get it," Lisa volunteered as quickly as she had the other time.

Her cup clattered noisily in its saucer as she set it down on the table and rose. But Slade's hand was on her forearm, stopping her with the punishing grip of his fingers.

"Mitzi will know exactly where it is," he said curtly.

"Maybe not exactly," her aunt qualified, "but I probably would have a better idea of where it is than Lisa. You two wait here while I look for it."

"Oh, no really," Lisa protested, a wildfire flaming hotly over her skin.

"Lisa," Slade muttered beneath his breath. In the use of her name there was a demanding order for her to stay.

"Come to think of it—" there was a decided twinkle

in Mitzi's eyes as she glanced at the two of them "—it may take me a little time to find that review."

Slade's piercing gaze never left Lisa's face. "I don't mind waiting, Mitzi."

CHAPTER SEVEN

WHEN MITZI HAD LEFT the room, Slade released Lisa's arm and took a hurried step away, turning his back to her. Lisa stared at the blackness of his hair brushing the rolled neckline of his ribbed, creamy yellow sweater, which complemented the tobacco-brown jacket of corduroy with light tan leather patches at the elbows.

"We both know you aren't here to read Mitzi's review, so why have you come, Slade?" Was that her voice that sounded so calm and nonchalant? It seemed impossible, considering the way she was trembling inside.

He slashed a black glance over his shoulder, brief and slicing. "It occurred to me that I was taking your agreement to our arrangement for granted. You avoided giving me a direct answer last night." Slade, too, sounded calm and controlled, yet the elemental currents crackling in the air seemed charged with high voltage.

"Did I? I thought I had," Lisa shrugged, intimidated by the rigid set of his shoulders.

Slade pivoted to face her. "You didn't and you haven't yet."

It was Lisa's turn to look away from his compelling

features, relentless in their demand for an answer. "Naturally, I agree to the arrangement. As you pointed out last night, it would be foolish and self-defeating for both of us not to join forces." Her attempt to be offhand came out brittle and defensive. "Is that direct enough for you, or do you want me to sign some binding document complete with the 'whereases' and 'hereinafters?'"

"Stop it!" he snapped out the words.

"Stop what?" Lisa turned on him roundly, more challengingly defensive than before.

"Stop being so sarcastic." A muscle worked convulsively along his lean jaw, the line of his mouth hard and forbidding.

"I can't help it where you're concerned," she restored. "It's instinctive."

"You managed to be civil last night," Slade reminded her.

"Last night I had too much wine," Lisa defended herself. It had been the crutch she had subconsciously used all day long to explain her reaction to his kisses.

"Was it the wine?" he taunted. "I've been wondering that myself all day long."

His admission caught her by surprise. She had been on his mind all day long? She was the reason for his moody preoccupation at the office? He had been going over in his mind what had happened the night before the same as she had. It must have been an unsettling experience for him as well. The knowledge quivered through her limbs, kindling an excitement she fought hard to control.

In one long stride, Slade covered the distance

between them, his hands spanning her slender ribcage. His touch sparked a flame that licked through her nervous system, making her insensitive to all but his nearness.

"I haven't had any wine today. Have you?" he asked with dangerous deliberation.

With a negative shake of her blond head, she gave him her mute answer. He slowly pulled her toward him. The hands on her ribs were firmly insisting, their searing warmth branding her skin. Her face was tipped upwards, her lips parting before he even touched them.

His questing mouth held no mercy, its fierce passion driving all resistance out of its path. The heady urgency he was arousing was more deeply intoxicating than any wine. Almost of their own accord, her hands slipped inside his jacket, sliding around the solidness of his waist.

Instantly his arms circled her, shaping her full curves to the hard contours of his body. The caress of his hands on her hips sent fires leaping high, consuming her with the scorching heat of their desire.

All men who had held her in her arms before were banished from her memory. None had ever lifted her to this towering peak that overlooked discretion and danger. The things she had resented about Slade, his strength and mastery, were the very things she now gloried in. She couldn't help shuddering in regret when he dragged his mouth from hers.

"What kind of a witch are you?" he muttered thickly against her temple, his breath warm and moist over her skin.

"A completely powerless one, I think." *Without*

resistance or defense, she thought silently. He could have seduced her and she wouldn't have been able to stop him.

His mouth punished her hard for telling such a lie. Only as far as Lisa was concerned, it wasn't a lie. Slade was the one who possessed the magic, trapping her inside the charmed circle of his arms while he wove a spell over her soul. She reveled in the addictive prowess of his long, drugging kiss, her need insatiable.

"Take off those damned glasses," Slade growled the demand.

It was the slap back to reality that Lisa needed. She twisted out of his arms, turning her back on him and taking a trembling step away. Her heart was knocking against her ribs, her breath coming in shaky gasps. She clasped her arms about her stomach, churning from the upheaval of her emotions, volcanic and frightening.

"I don't want to become involved with you, Slade, emotionally or physically," she declared, but much too weakly. "I want this to be purely a business arrangement." Eventually she would have to expose him, and she wanted to be able to do it without pain or regret.

"Do you think I don't?" His low voice sounded strangled by the savage control he was exercising over his reply.

"I don't know," she sighed with an aching tremor.

His hands touched the sides of her waist, then slid automatically under her arms to cup her breasts. Lisa's shoulders were drawn back against his chest. The hard pressure of his thighs left her in no doubt of his male need.

"I didn't intend for this to happen. In fact, it's the last thing I want." Even as he made the angry statement, he was forcing her head to the side, burying his mouth in the tangle of silver silk hair at the curve of her neck.

"Me, too." But delicious shivers were racing down her spine from his rough caress.

Her hands were clutching his muscled forearms, ostensibly to end his possession of her breasts. But she simply held on to him, inviting his intimate caress by not denying it. A wave of primitive longings surged through her—powerful, inescapable and dangerous.

"It's happened, so what are we going to do about it?" Slade breathed raggedly against the sensitive skin along her neck.

"Stop it."

"Can you?" he laughed cynically.

"I don't know." Lisa closed her eyes against the fevered ache in her loins that refused to diminish.

Tightening his hold, he molded her more fully against his male length. "I want you, Lisa." A hand slid to her hipbone.

"I know." How could she ignore the pressing force of his desire, any more than she could ignore the hollow throbbing of her own?

Abruptly Slade let her go, leaving her to sway unsteadily without the support of his body. Long, impatient strides carried him away from her until nearly the width of the room separated them. Lisa stared hungrily after him, not able to deny her desire now that he no longer held her in his arms.

He took a cigarette from the enameled box on the

coffee table and snapped a lighter flame to the tip. Exhaling an impatient, tasteless cloud of smoke, he raked his fingers through the thickness of his raven hair. The smoldering anger of his gaze burned her.

"What do you expect from me, Lisa?" he demanded with gritting control. "Besides a guaranteed share of your aunt's money," he jeered viciously.

"Nothing." Hot tears scorched her eyes, luckily hidden by the smoke blue sunglasses. "God, I wish I'd never met you!" she choked.

"Not half as much as I do," he growled. "Not by half!"

The just-lit cigarette was crushed in an ashtray, suppressed fury in the action. He was striding stiffly toward the door before Lisa could comprehend his intention.

"Where are you going?" she breathed in confusion.

"I'm leaving!" he snapped harshly. "Make my apologies to your aunt!"

Doors were slammed violently in his wake. Lisa flinched at each crashing sound, pain splintering through her, inflicting a million tiny wounds.

It was what she deserved, though, for so indiscriminately abandoning her pride and self-respect in the arms of a man who was a thief and possibly worse. There was no time to dwell on the humiliating aspects of her passionate response as Mitzi appeared in the living room.

"Gracious! Slade was really in a temper when he left," she declared. "I can't leave the two of you alone for five minutes but you're at each other's throats. What happened this time?"

"We—argued," Lisa answered tightly, her voice straining to sound natural.

"About what?"

"Does it matter?" she countered with undisguised bitterness.

"I suppose not," Mitzi sighed in reluctant agreement. "You two can't seem to see eye to eye about anything. If all else failed, you'd probably argue over the color of the sun. After last night, I'd hoped that—"

"Last night was a mistake." In more ways than one, Lisa could have told her. A fiery tear slipped from her lashes and she wiped it away with the back of her hand.

"Lisa, you're crying!" Mitzi was plainly astonished by the discovery.

"I always cry when I'm angry." *Or hurt or confused or frightened,* she thought.

Her aunt's expression became decidedly grim. "I am going to have a talk with Slade."

"Don't bother. He'd only laugh," Lisa declared acidly.

"Slade—"

"You don't know Slade," Lisa interrupted angrily, releasing the pent-up frustrations of her emotions. "You don't know what he's really like! How arrogant and demanding and sexy—" Oh, God, Lisa thought. Had she really said that last? She went red with shame.

"Well, no—" Mitzi tried to hide the laughter in her voice "—I don't think I know that side of him very well."

Lisa couldn't remember having felt so mortified in years, not since a teenage girl friend had confided

Lisa's infatuation to the very boy she had the crush on. She mumbled some unintelligible excuse and rushed from the room.

In her room, she locked the door, but no one came to invade her privacy. She cried out her misery and humiliation alone. But it was more than that that made her sob so brokenly with pain. It was knowing that she had found something precious and couldn't keep it.

But she refused to admit, even to herself, what that something precious was. With her head pounding and her body aching, she finally fell into an exhausted sleep some time after midnight.

The next morning, Lisa awoke with a start. She was late for work. Then her head sank back onto the pillow. It was Saturday and Slade's office was closed. Relief trembled through her in a shuddering sigh. She would never have found the composure to face Slade today as Ann Eldridge.

A glance in the mirror told her she would have difficulty facing anyone today. Her green eyes were parched and bloodshot from the gallons of tears she had cried. Her lids were puffy and swollen with dark smudges beneath her eyes. She could hardly stand to see herself.

She slipped on her sunglasses to conceal the ravages of last night's stormy collapse. Only when the worst had been hidden did she pull on brushed denim Levis and a white tank top. Her complexion was unnaturally pale, making the pink lipstick look gaudy. She rubbed it off with a tissue and ran a comb indifferently through her silver blond hair.

Downstairs the housekeeper gave her a sighingly

resigned look and said, "Mitzi is in the study working. Today is the day I polish the furniture, so if you'll be wantin' breakfast, it'll take me a while."

"Juice and coffee is good enough." Lisa still didn't have an appetite. Mildred nodded glumly, showing no relief that the request was small. "I'll get it," Lisa volunteered. "There's no need for you to bother, Mildred."

"Have it your way." Mildred shrugged and moved toward the living room.

In the end, Lisa had only a glass of orange juice before wandering aimlessly out of the back door into the garden. Listlessly she meandered under the large oaks, veils of moss trailing over the top of her hair.

Last night she had considered packing her bags and leaving—anything to escape Slade Blackwell. But that would mean leaving Mitzi to his mercy. Was she such a coward she would do that?

But if she stayed . . . . Lisa shuddered. She was supposed to be an adult, not without some experience regarding men. She should be capable of warding off unwanted attentions from a man. The problem was that they were not unwanted. All Slade had to do was touch her and she melted like a scoop of ice cream in July.

Never, not even in her worst nightmares, had she dreamed she might fall in love with a man who embezzled from rich, elderly women. She hadn't fallen in love with him yet; in lust with him maybe, but not in love.

But that was the risk she was taking if she stayed around him much longer, Lisa realized. And if she loved him, would she have the will to expose him before he destroyed Mitzi's future security?

She was so confused and uncertain. Nothing seemed as simple as it had when she arrived. A twig of an oak brushed her cheek and she snapped it off in irritation, twirling the tiny, green-leafed stick between her fingers agitatedly.

What was she going to do? How had she got herself into this mess? How was she going to get herself out of it? Was there a way out of it—one that wasn't filled with pain or heartache?

Sighing helplessly, Lisa tipped her head backward, gazing up into the massive branches of an oak tree. Far above her head she could see a man-made platform perched on the V of two limbs. She searched the fat girth of the main trunk, finding the slats of wood nailed to the tree forming a crude ladder to the platform.

It looked singularly inviting to be high up there in the tree, far above all her problems. The lofty treehouse offered a temporary escape, and Lisa took advantage of it. The boards nailed to the trunk were amazingly solid. Even if they hadn't been, she discovered that she hadn't lost her climbing skill. The platform, too, was sound, without a single indication of rotting wood.

Settling into a comfortable, cross-legged position, with her elbows resting on her thighs and her hands on her ankles, Lisa felt decidedly better. There was something uplifting about sitting in a tree. If Darwin's theory was true, she thought somewhat wryly, she was probably reverting to old ancestral habits!

The sensation didn't last long as she heard the crunch of footsteps in the graveled driveway. She tensed, a sixth sense warning her of the intruder's identity before she saw Slade. The minute he came into her view, he stopped, glancing upward to the treehouse where she sat.

Her heart somersaulted traitorously at the sight of him dressed casually in blue slacks and a print shirt that was opened at the throat. His hard features were expressionless as he gazed directly at her.

"Go away," she gulped tightly.

"I want to talk to you, Lisa," he said evenly.

"Well, I don't want to talk to you."

"Don't be childish," Slade scolded her for her pouting retort, "and come down from that tree."

"How did you know I was here?" She ignored his order.

"Mildred told me at the house that she'd seen you wandering around outside from the window. I've found Mitzi so many times in that treehouse that I guess I automatically looked there first."

"Mitzi? Up here?" Lisa repeated, finding it difficult to imagine her fifty-year-old aunt climbing the tree.

"Yes," Slade said dryly, "your aunt is remarkable in more ways than one. If you don't come down, I'll come up. You'll find that platform is a little cramped with two people on it."

He would climb up, Lisa knew it, and she glared at him angrily. He took a step toward the trunk and the crude ladder.

"I'll be right down," she muttered, and slid along the platform to the boards leading down the tree.

A few feet from the ground, a pair of hands took hold of her waist, ignoring her gasp of protest, and lifted her the rest of the way down. Lisa twisted free of the hold the instant her feet touched the ground. Her pulse was still racing even after Slade had let her go.

"What do you want?" she challenged coldly. But inside she was feverishly aware of him.

Slade stared at her for a long moment. "Mitzi told me you'd been crying."

His hand reached for her sunglasses and Lisa knocked it away, instinctively defending her identity. "She had no right to tell you that!" She couldn't deny the tears she had cried. Not even the tinted sunglasses could conceal all traces.

"Mitzi hasn't had many chances in her life to play mother hen. You can't blame her for springing to the defense of the little chick living in her house." He studied her thoughtfully. "Looking at you now, I can understand why she lectured me on my behavior. You look oddly vulnerable and in need of protection."

"You're wrong," Lisa denied. "You and Mitzi both are wrong. I can take care of myself."

"Can you?" Slade eyed her skeptically, his manner faintly arrogant and mocking. "It's funny, but you don't look like a hard-bitten little niece out after her aunt's money. You look like a little girl who's been hurt—"

"Will you get out of here?" she demanded hoarsely. "I don't need pity, least of all yours!"

"I'm not offering any."

Lisa turned away in agitation. "What are you doing here? Who invited you anyway?"

"I invited myself. I wanted to see you."

"Why?" she hurled bitterly. "Were you afraid after last night that I'd renege on our deal?"

"Frankly it didn't occur to me," Slade answered grimly. "Maybe it should have."

"Yes, maybe it should have."

His hands fastened on her upper arms, pulling her around to face him. Lisa hunched her shoulders away from him, recoiling from his touch that was both torture and bliss. She kept her face averted, unable to meet his compelling gaze.

"Let me go Slade!" The strangled words were ripped from her throat. "I'm not going to go back on our agreement."

His fingers curled deeper into the soft flesh of her arms, drawing her closer. Lisa raised her hands to wedge herself away from his chest, but one hand accidentally came in contact with naked skin where his unbuttoned shirt front opened at the neck. His body warmth seared through her like a branding iron, and the dark hairs on his chest tickled her sensitive fingertips.

"Last night—" Slade began tautly.

"I'm trying to forget about last night," Lisa interrupted in a throbbing voice. "I don't want to remember it even happened."

"I came over here this morning with the intention of apologizing and to suggest that we both forget about last night." There was a sensual note in his husky tone. "But I can't. It isn't possible."

His warm breath was fanning the top of her hair, letting Lisa know how close he was to her. Her gaze was riveted to the tanned column of his neck, and the pulse beating wildly there seemed to be in tempo with her own racing heart.

"I don't want to become involved with you." Her protest was almost issued in a moan of surrender. "It would complicate everything."

"Do you think I don't know that?" Slade argued grimly.

"Then leave me alone."

He offered the opposite. "Spend the day with me, Lisa. Mitzi's going to be working and she's already told me you aren't seeing your friends today."

"No." She shook her head. "I can't. I won't!"

"We won't talk about Mitzi or her money," Slade vowed. "We'll forget all about it. It'll just be you and me together."

The temptation to accept was almost irresistible. To have one day with Slade—to be just a man and a woman together—was a tantalizing thought.

"No!" The denial came in a tortured whisper, trembling with regret.

"You crazy, stubborn woman," he snapped in irritation. "You were human enough to cry last night. Can't you see that whether I like it or not, I'm falling in love with you?"

Lisa breathed in sharply, her head jerking up to stare dazedly into his face. His compelling features were set in grim, forbidding lines of determination.

"You can't mean it," she breathed.

His mouth twisted wryly. "Do you think it was easy for me to admit or accept?"

"I don't know." She wavered. "You can't love me," she protested uncertainly.

"That's what I've been saying ever since I left the house last night," Slade admitted, a rueful smile tugging cynically at the corners of his mouth. "But I know the worst about you, Lisa. Today I'd like to find out the best."

Yes, it was true for her, too. She knew the worst about Slade—that he was dishonest, an embezzler—but it didn't change the way she felt about him. The difference between Lisa and Slade was that she was afraid to pin the label of love on the emotion she felt. In her heart she was certain, but her mind refused to accept the verdict.

"It wouldn't change anything. It would only make it worse." She couldn't bring herself to accept his invitation.

"I don't know." He lifted an expressive brow in challenge. "I might find your company boring without any arguments to add spice."

Lisa held her breath for an instant, then released it in a long sigh. "No, I can't go."

"Why?" Slade demanded a reason.

"It's—it's too risky," she offered lamely.

"Why? Because you might find out you're in love with me?" he guessed astutely. "Is there a chance of that?"

Moistening her lips nervously, Lisa finally admitted, "Yes."

The smoldering light that leaped into his dark eyes took her breath away. "If there's a chance of that," he said tightly, "we can find out right here and now."

Her lips parted to protest, but his mouth opened over hers to silence her voice, devouring her lips with a savage hunger that brought sweet pain. Lisa surrendered instantly to the fierce ecstasy of his kiss. Her arms slid around his neck inside his shirt collar, feeling the flexing of his muscles as he crushed her against his length.

The erotic stimulation in the molding caress of his hands drove out all questions about the wisdom of loving him. There was only here and now and the wonder of his arms around her. Her heart was singing a pagan song to accompany the primitive fires racing through her veins. The sensual probe of his lips as they explored hers had her quivering in eager response, needing to know him as intimately as he was discovering her.

His weight pressed her backward until the rough bark of the tree was rasping her shoulder blades and the bare skin exposed by the sleeveless tank top. A muscular leg was forced between hers as Slade pinned her arching body against the trunk. His hands slipped under the hem of her top, finding the heat of her bare skin and evoking a pleasure so piercing it was near torment.

Her breast seemed to swell in delight when his hand curved over the lacy cup of her bra. Lisa yearned to feel the nakedness of his hard flesh beneath her fingers. Lacking his expertise, her fingers fumbled with the few remaining buttons of his shirt. In her awkward attempt, she scraped her elbow against the rough bark and gasped at the sharp pain shooting up her arm.

Slade immediately straightened, pulling her with him away from the tree. "This is a hell of a place to make love to you," he laughed raggedly near her ear, nuzzling its lobe before dragging his mouth away.

Weakly Lisa rested her head against his chest, still quivering with a need that could only be satisfied in the consummation of their love. Unknowingly she whispered his name.

"Love me?" Slade roughly demanded an answer.

"Yes." And she closed her eyes at the frightening truth.

"And you'll spend the day with me?"

Lisa trembled. "Yes."

His arms tightened around her. "Do you have any idea how much I want you?"

"I think so," she nodded against his chest, her fingers spreading across his hard flesh in an unconscious caress. She knew how much she wanted him.

"It's so soon, though," Slade declared in agitation, rubbing his chin over the top of her head. Lisa could hear the frown in his voice. "Is there ever a right time and a right place?"

"I doubt it."

He captured her chin and lifted her head so he could study her face, his eyes darkened in seriousness. "Lisa, I want to spend the afternoon getting to know you—I don't mean physically, there's time enough for that later. I want to know about your family and friends, what you like and what you don't like."

"Yes." She seemed destined to agree with anything he said, but it wouldn't last forever. Maybe that was why she was clinging so tenaciously to those few moments they would share.

He gave her a hard, swift kiss. "It's not going to be easy to keep my hands off of you when you're in such a delectable mood, but I'll try," he promised in lazy arrogance. "As long as you don't provoke me." Clasping her wrists, he held her away from him. "Run into the house and let Mildred know you're coming with me. I'll have you back in time for dinner tonight."

"Should I change? I mean—" Lisa glanced down at the rumpled tank top and snug-fitting Levis.

"You're fine as you are," he assured her.

"All right," she nodded tightly. "Just give me five minutes to comb my hair and put on some lipstick."

"No." His grip tightened when she would have pulled free of his light hold to go to the house. Lisa looked back into his disturbing intent gaze. "No comb and no lipstick. I want you looking just the way you are—as if you'd just been kissed very thoroughly by me."

"Slade, what will people think?" She was faintly embarrassed yet thrilled by the possessive ring in his voice.

"They'll think we're in love," he informed her with more than a trace of arrogant satisfaction, "and that I've made mad, passionate love to you. I haven't, but I will."

"Oh, really?" Lisa had to challenge him. She had been much too agreeable.

"Yes, really." For an instant, he drew her against his chest as if to establish his mastery over her. "And if you don't hurry into the house with that message, I'll change the order in which I want to get to know you better." Then he released her.

"Damn you, Slade!" she breathed, standing motionless, loving him and hating him with equal desperation. "The first thing you should learn about me is that I don't like being told what to do."

"Very well." Amusement deepened the corners of his mouth. "I won't tell you what to do any more. I'll show you."

Taking her by the shoulders, he turned her around and pointed her toward the house. With a shove and a playful slap on her rump, he sent her on her way.

Entering the house through the back door, Lisa went in search of Mitzi. In the foyer, she heard the clicking keys of the typewriter in the study. Hesitating, Lisa decided not to disturb her aunt and began looking for the housekeeper.

After going through all the rooms but the study on the ground floor, Lisa continued her search upstairs. She found Mildred in her bedroom, polishing the chest of drawers.

"Here you are, Mildred." She was slightly out of breath. "I've been looking for you."

"I always polish the furniture upstairs first," Mildred informed her. "I don't know why I bother. Nobody hardly ever comes up here. I'm just wasting my time." She pulled out a drawer and ran a cloth around the edges and sides. "But it has to be done. So I do it first. That way I leave the downstairs till last and I have to do that. I can't put it off because somebody is always running in and out."

Lisa wasn't really interested in hearing Mildred's psychological methods of keeping house. "Slade is here and—"

"Yes, I know. I answered the door when he rang the bell. As if I haven't got anything better to do than run up and down stairs seeing who is at the door," she grumbled.

"Yes, well, I came to tell you that he's asked me to

spend the day with him." Not even the housekeeper's grouchiness could diminish the happiness Lisa felt at the prospect of spending an entire day with Slade. "I'll be back in time for dinner tonight."

"And I've got a casserole in the oven for lunch," Mildred grumped and opened another drawer. In alarm, she stepped away from it with surprising swiftness. "What is that thing in there?" she demanded. "It looks like some furry animal."

Lisa realized which drawer Mildred had opened and went white. "It isn't an animal," she started to explain but Mildred was already reaching a tentative hand into the drawer to touch it.

"It's hair!" she exclaimed in a mixture of bewilderment and irritation.

"It's a wig," Lisa identified it.

"A wig?" The housekeeper took it out of the drawer to examine it more closely. "You didn't have a wig when I unpacked your things. What would you want with a wig? And a red one, at that?"

The woman's attitude made Lisa feel as guilty as if she'd stolen it. "I . . . I bought it to play a joke on somebody." It was difficult to look the housekeeper in the eye and lie. "And I guess I always wondered what I'd look like in red hair."

"It's a waste of money if you ask me." Mildred sniffed in disapproval as she stuffed the wig back in the drawer.

Lisa inched toward the door. She didn't want to think about Ann Eldridge or anything about the reason she had come to Charleston, not today.

"You will tell Mitzi where I've gone?" she reminded the housekeeper that she was leaving.

"I'll tell her." The woman reached for the bottle of furniture polish, but it was empty. "Now I've got to make another trip downstairs. This just isn't my day," she complained aloud.

"Slade is waiting for me. I have to go." Lisa turned to leave the room, and Mildred was right behind her.

At the bottom of the stairs, Mildred spoke up. "I still don't understand why you'd want to buy a red wig when you have such beautiful hair."

"I told you I just did it for the fun of it," Lisa retorted impatiently, anxious to have the subject dropped before it infringed on her happiness.

"It's nothing to me how you spend your money," Mildred shrugged her slouching shoulders and turned down the hallway to the kitchen.

At that moment Slade rounded the corner, his dark gaze lighting on Lisa. "Your five minutes are up. Are you coming?"

"Yes." She almost dashed past Mildred to reach him and get him out of the house before the woman said any more about what she'd found in Lisa's drawer.

If Slade had appeared only a few minutes sooner, he would have discovered all about her deception. Lisa dreaded the moment when he would find out, not because she hadn't obtained the evidence she wanted, but because of what it would mean personally.

Outside, Slade helped her into the passenger side of the car. "I almost wish your answer had been no, you weren't coming," he said, pausing beside the car before he closed her door.

"Why?" She held her breath, her expression inscrutable.

"Because then I could have persuaded you to change

your mind all over again." A half smile curved the hard, male line of his mouth.

Lisa released the breath in silent relief as he closed her door and walked around to the driver's side. A little voice inside her head said she was being a fool, but she ignored it.

CHAPTER EIGHT

THE REST OF THE MORNING and afternoon was spent driving. As Slade put it, if he had to keep his concentration on the road, he would be less tempted to take back his statement that they would just talk.

They traversed the whole Low Country area of South Carolina located around Charleston, stopping at noon to lunch in a crowded restaurant and again in midafternoon for a cold drink.

Lisa didn't remember the last time she had told anyone so much about herself. But then they had both talked a great deal. The subjects had ranged from their childhood, their family and friends, to their work and hobbies, the kind of musing they liked and the books they read. Yet they both carefully avoided the subject of Mitzi Talmadge.

Myrtle Beach and the Golden Strand were far behind them now. Each rotation of the tires was taking them closer to Charleston. It was inevitable that the afternoon had to end. Staring at the Highway 17 sign at the side of the road, Lisa realized it and wished they were sixty miles from Charleston instead of six. Unconsciously she sighed in regret.

"What's wrong?" Perceptively Slade had caught the small sound and let his gaze be distracted briefly from the highway.

"Nothing," Lisa insisted, but she knew he would persist if she didn't divert his attention. "There must be a boom in baskets. I've never seen so many stands along the road selling them. Just look at them!"

"Surely you've seen them before?" he frowned.

"No, I haven't."

"But you had to come this way to get to Brookgreen Gardens." He was eyeing her curiously.

"Oh," she laughed self-consciously, "I guess we were talking so much we never noticed any roadstands. You know how it is when a bunch of girls get together. Peg, Susan and I are no different."

Slade nodded and Lisa knew she had covered her fabrication story of having been to Brookgreen Gardens and how she had missed seeing these stands.

"You mustn't have heard about our Low Country coil baskets." He slowed the car and turned off the road, stopping in front of one of the stands. "Coil basketry is an African art brought over here by the slaves. The skill and designs have been passed down from one generation to another, sometimes with new designs by new artists being introduced along the way. Come on and we'll take a look. We can't have your education neglected," he mocked gently.

With Slade at her side, Lisa inspected the roadside display. The baskets came in all shapes and sizes, some intricate in their designs, some plain, some with lids and some open.

An aging black woman sat in a chair to one side of the stand, a sweater around her shoulders. Her nimble fingers were busy creating the coiled base of another basket, but not too busy that she was unaware of Slade and Lisa looking over her display.

"Generally women make the show baskets," Slade explained, "and men make the sturdier work baskets that were, and in some cases still are, used for agricultural purposes."

He pointed out a large, very shallow basket, called a "fanner basket," used to winnow rice, which was once the main crop of the large plantations around Charleston because of the high water table of the Low Country. Lisa picked up a smaller basket to study it more closely.

"The craftsmanship is superb," she murmured more to herself than to Slade. "How do they make them? What do they use?"

"The show baskets use sweet grass sewn together with the split leaf of the palmetto palm. The dark stripes in some of the baskets are decorations made by long needles of pine straw." He showed her the stitches of the palmetto leaf that seemed to radiate out in a straight line from the center of the coil basket. "The work baskets use bulrushes and split white oak or split palmetto butt for more strength."

"The materials are found locally?"

"Once they were in great abundance, but that isn't as true today. Large tracts of land where the sweet grass and palmetto palm grew have been developed into housing or resort areas. It's becoming more difficult for the basket artists to find natural materials for their work because of it." He glanced at the basket in her hand. "Would you like to have that?"

"Yes, it's beautiful, but—" Lisa started to point out that she had no money with her.

"My first gift to you." Slade didn't let her finish as he

gently pried the basket from her fingers and walked over to the elderly artist to pay for it.

A few minutes later they were back on the road heading toward Charleston. Lisa held the small coil basket in her lap. Her first gift from Slade. He had said it as if it would be the first of many.

But whose money would pay for them? His or Mitzi's? She stared out of the window, wishing she hadn't thought of that. It spoiled her pleasure in the gift and, somehow, the day.

Neither of them spoke in the last half dozen miles to Mitzi's house. Lisa gazed absently out of the window, lost in her melancholy thoughts, and Slade had to concentrate on the traffic that got heavier as they entered the city limits of Charleston.

The scrolled wrought-iron gates were open to admit them to the driveway of Mitzi's house. Slade stopped the car in front of the portico and switched off the motor. Without a word, he climbed out of the car and walked around to Lisa's door.

"We're here," he announced unnecessarily as he opened it.

"Yes." Her reply was as instant as his comment.

They both seemed caught in the web of tension between them. Walking to the carved entrance doors of the house, Lisa attempted to brush it away.

"Did I bore you this afternoon?" She tried to be light and teasing, but there was an anxious note in the question.

"I don't know when I've been so—bored with a woman in my life," Slade mocked.

Lisa glanced away, a painful tightness in her throat. "Don't make jokes, Slade."

"Don't ask stupid questions, Lisa," he returned.

At the door she turned, her hand poised on the knob, straining for composure and wishing she didn't feel as if she was leaving him for good.

"Will you come in for a few minutes?"

"No." Slade leaned an arm against the jamb, effectively blocking her from entering the house immediately.

His dark head bent toward her and Lisa moved forward to meet him. The delicate violence in his kiss told her how great his restraint had been all day as he released the passion he had controlled. His desire wasn't satiated by the assault on her lips nor the feel of her pliant body arching to mold itself against the hard contours of his.

"I've been wanting to do that all day," he said, dragging his hard mouth from her lips to nuzzle the lobe of her ear. "That and more."

Her one free hand was exploring the rough texture of his face while the other still crazily held on to the basket. Eyes closed against the sweet torment of loving him and not knowing the culmination of that love, Lisa pressed herself closer to his length. She quivered with longing as he explored the base of her neck and the hollow of her throat, finding her pleasure points with seductive ease.

"Slade, I don't want you to ever let me go." The trembling plea was issued in fear.

His mouth broke off the burning contact with her bare skin as he crushed her in the iron circle of his arms. She felt the inner shudder of longing he tried to conceal.

"Come over to my apartment tonight," he ordered in a voice that was husky and raw.

"I—can't," Lisa denied achingly.

"Yes, you can." His arms tightened punishingly around her. "After dinner, you can leave Mitzi alone with her coffee. Or come after she's gone to bed—I don't care."

"No!" She shook her head, wanting desperately to agree.

"Damnit, Lisa—" Slade began angrily as if tortured, his need for her surpassing his endurance.

"I'm not a prude, Slade," Lisa answered shakily. "But I can't do that to Mitzi. She may be open-minded, but she would never approve of that."

"You're right." He breathed in deeply, fighting for control as he loosened his hold. "The mother hen would feel overly responsible for her adopted chick. If you spent the night with me, we could never convince her that she hadn't failed you somehow. It would be foolish to hurt her that way."

"Yes," Lisa agreed with sudden bitterness, "we don't want her thinking badly of us."

Inwardly she damned her aunt's money and Slade's greed for it. He claimed to love her, but not even for love would he risk losing his chance for Mitzi's wealth. It cheapened her feeling for him somehow.

"Tomorrow—" Slade began, sliding his hands caressingly along her spine.

Lisa knew she didn't dare see him or spend time with him Sunday. "Tomorrow I'll have to devote to Mitzi," she insisted. "Since I've been here, I've hardly been with her at all. I can't go running off again or she'll think I've come here just to have free room and board on my vacation."

Slade seemed about to argue, then changed his mind. "Okay, I'll see you Monday. We'll have dinner and—" a tight smile quirked his mouth as he lifted his head to look at her "—we'll see what else."

"Yes," Lisa agreed with a strained smile, a terrible depression settling over her. "I'd better be going in." She firmly disentangled herself from his embrace and turned to the door. He didn't try to stop her. "Good night, Slade," she murmured, aware that he hadn't moved.

"Lisa." It was a husky demand to come back to his arms.

At the feathery brush of his fingers against the spun silver strands of her hair, Lisa wrenched open the door and bolted inside. Closing the door, she leaned against it, the pain of loving him choking her throat. Seconds later she heard the slamming of the car door and the starting growl of the engine.

The weekend dragged slowly by for Lisa. By Monday morning, the strain of being bright, supposedly untroubled company for Mitzi was beginning to show in her pale features. While Lisa was walking to Slade's office, she debated whether she was going to carry out her masquerade as Ann Eldridge for another day. The affirmative answer was inescapable. She had to find out the extent of Slade's treachery.

Drew followed her into the office when she arrived. "A redhead in basic black. I can't think of a more striking combination than that," he declared with a wolfish smile.

"Flattery will get you absolutely nowhere with me." She ran a perspiring palm over the hip of her black pantsuit.

The box-style jacket was a reversible green plaid. Lisa wished now she had chosen to wear that side out instead of the black. She would have felt less like being in mourning.

"Not even an acceptance of my lunch invitation?"

"No," she refused.

She was much too tense to make small talk over a sandwich, even if the noon hour was three hours away. Her taut condition was unlikely to improve.

"I don't think you're ever going to say yes," Drew sighed.

The outer office door swung open and Slade came striding in. Vitality radiated from him with the blinding force of direct sunlight, and Lisa was glad she was sitting in her chair. The sight of him made her weak, especially when he walked directly to her desk and flashed her one of his devastating smiles.

"Good morning, Mrs. Eldridge, Drew." He picked up the morning mail sitting in the basket on her desk and began glancing through it, a trace of the smile still curving the hard line of his mouth.

"Good morning, Mr. Blackwell." Lisa had to lower her gaze to keep from devouring him with her eyes.

Drew whistled softly. "Introduce me to her, Slade."

"To whom?" Slade tipped his head curiously at his close friend and associate, the half smile not leaving his mouth.

"To the girl who made your weekend so bright that it carried over to Monday morning. She must be special to make you this cheerful," Drew declared, so intent on Slade that he missed the rush of color that rouged Lisa's cheeks. "I want to meet her."

"Not a chance." A rich, throaty laugh came from Slade, sending delicious shivers over Lisa's skin. "She's all mine and I intend to keep it that way."

When Slade disappeared into his office, Drew turned to Lisa, his eyes widening suggestively. "I get the feeling Cupid has struck. I swear I saw a whole quiver of arrows sticking out of his back. I don't know who's luckier, Slade or the girl."

A warm glow brightened the green of her eyes. "Both, I hope." It was almost a silent prayer that it could be so.

"Slade's caught the golden ring and you've turned me down for lunch," Drew shook his head. "I couldn't feel more left out if I was locked in a tower with the key thrown away."

"Your turn will come," Lisa offered.

"Yeah," he agreed glumly. "In the meantime, back to the 'blue Monday' salt mines!"

Drew had barely left Lisa's office when Slade walked back in from his, carrying a stack of papers and folders which he dumped on her desk.

"Here," he said. "You can file these this morning, Ann," he added, using her supposed given name unconsciously before turning to reenter his office.

"What about those contracts you said last Friday had to be typed first thing this morning?" Lisa reminded him.

He paused at his door, a recklessly indifferent look carved in his compelling features. "Forget it," he shrugged with uncharacteristic disregard for the contracts' importance. "Typing isn't one of your favorite things, and the day is too beautiful to be clouded by drudgery. The contracts can wait till another day."

Her mouth opened in disbelief, but Slade was already closing his door, not seeming to realize how unlike himself he was behaving. Yet it left Lisa in little doubt that he really loved her. With a happy smile, she turned toward the stack of filing to be done.

Black letters seemed to leap from the tab of one of the folders and her heart stopped beating for a split second. "Talmadge, Miriam," the letters spelled.

With shaking fingers, Lisa pulled the folder out of the stack, staring at it almost in dread. It was what she had been waiting for—to have Mitzi's file in her possession. She closed her eyes weakly, wishing it hadn't happened.

The telephone rang shrilly in her ears. Lisa hesitated, then quickly slipped the folder in a desk drawer and answered the phone. When she had transferred the call to Slade, she ignored the closed desk drawer. Picking up the stack of papers and folders, she carried them to the metal cabinets, setting them on top of one of them and systematically began filing them in the proper place.

She had not completely mastered the filing system. She still relied heavily on the guess and search method. In consequence, an hour later there was one-third of the stack yet to be filed when Slade emerged from his office.

"I'll be gone for about twenty minutes if anyone's

looking for me," he told her, still with that contented light burning in his dark eyes.

"Yes, Mr. Blackwell," she nodded.

With the closing of the door, she walked back to her desk, sat down in her chair and stared at the desk drawer. She clenched her hands tightly in her lap, then tore them apart to reach for the telephone, finding a reason to stall the inevitable for a few more minutes.

When she'd left the house that morning, she hadn't said where she was going nor how long she would be gone because she hadn't been sure she would come to the office. She djaled Mitzi's number, fabricating another story in her mind as to why she wouldn't be home until early evening.

"Talmadge residence." The call was answered on the second ring.

"Mildred, this is—" she began.

"Lisa, is that you?" It was Mitzi who was on the phone instead of the housekeeper.

"Yes, it is," Lisa rushed nervously. "I was cal—"

"I'm so glad you called," Mitzi interrupted her again. "Exactly sixteen minutes ago I typed those six magic letters."

"What?" she asked blankly.

Mitzi laughed. "'The End.' I've finished my new novel!"

"That's wonderful," Lisa agreed with forced enthusiasm.

"It's heavenly!" her aunt gushed. "And it calls for an immediate celebration. Where are you? I'll meet you for lunch at some frightfully swank restaurant."

Her heart sank. "Well, actually, Mitzi, I'm—"

"Oh, no, don't tell me you can't make it." Mitzi sounded genuinely crushed. "If you're with your two friends, bring them along. We'll make a party of it."

"No, no, they can't make it." Lisa rubbed her hand across her forehead, feeling the beginnings of a headache start to pound in her temples. She just couldn't disappoint her aunt. "But I can meet you at noon. Where would you like to celebrate?"

Mitzi suggested a restaurant that was fortunately within walking distance of the office, and Lisa agreed. Her aunt sounded quite jubilant when Lisa hung up, while she sighed dispiritedly. She opened the desk drawer to take out Mitzi's folder and Drew walked in. She closed the drawer with guilty swiftness.

"Aha! I caught you doing your fingernails, didn't I?" he accused with mock anger. "If you don't have lunch with me, I'll tell Slade."

"You're out of luck. He isn't here," Lisa retorted with false brightness.

"Where did he go?" Drew grimaced.

"He didn't say. All he told me is that he would be back in twenty minutes." She shrugged, and rose from the desk to return to the filing.

"Well—" Drew breathed in deeply and shoved his hands in his pockets "—I guess I'll keep you company until he comes back." He wandered over to the cabinets where Lisa worked. "What are you doing?"

"Filing. Want to help?" she offered.

"No, thanks," he smiled, and eyed her lazily. "So you won't give in to my blackmail and have lunch with me?"

"No," Lisa repeated her earlier refusal.

"It's just as well, I suppose. Considering the benevolent mood Slade is in, he'd probably send you out for a manicure if I told him I'd caught you doing your nails. Not that they need doing." He caught one of her hands and refused to let it go. "Everything about you is beautiful, Ann, including your nails. No wonder you can't type," he said, touching the rounded length of one of her nails.

"Now you know my darkest secret." Lisa firmly pulled her hand from his grasp just as Slade returned.

"No holding hands during office hours," he scolded laughingly. "Her husband is going to show up here one day, Drew, and you're going to be in trouble."

The telephone rang, interrupting Drew's reply. Lisa started toward her desk, but Slade waved her away. "I'll answer it." He picked up the receiver. "Slade Blackwell," he identified himself briskly, and Lisa turned back to the cabinet, resisting the desire to gaze at him. "Hello, Mitzi, how are you?"

Lisa froze, the folder in her hand poised above the open cabinet drawer, her fingers tightening whitely as they gripped the stiff paper.

"It goes here," Drew whispered, indicating a spot between two file folders already in the drawer. She shoved the folder between them.

"You did?" Slade was speaking again. "Congratulations....Lunch today?"

He seemed to hesitate and Lisa pivoted quickly toward him. "You have an appointment for lunch, Mr. Blackwell," she reminded him, hoping she didn't sound as panicked as she felt.

Slade glanced at her briefly, then smiled suddenly at

the mouthpiece. "She's meeting you at noon? Of course I'll be there, Mitzi."

"What about your appointment?" Lisa accused frantically when he hung up the telephone.

"Who was it with?" He glanced at the day's calendar with remarkable unconcern. "Art Jones? Call him up and change it to another day."

"*She* is going to be there." Drew stressed the feminine pronoun suggestively.

Slade flashed him a glittering look, his dark eyes sparkling with an inner brilliance. "I'm not inviting you along, Drew. It's bad enough that her aunt is going to be there, without having you, too."

"Nobody wants to eat lunch with me," Drew declared with mock exasperation.

"Too bad," Slade chuckled quietly. "Did you want to see me about something, Drew, or are you here just to give Ann a bad time?"

"No, there's something I want to discuss with you. That is, if you think you can concentrate on business for five minutes and forget your girl," was the teasing answer.

"Mr. Blackwell?" Lisa heard herself asking for his attention.

He turned, absently curious. "Yes?"

"I have a dental appointment over the noon hour," she lied. "Would it be all right if I left a little early?"

"Of course."

A few minutes past the appointment meeting time, Lisa walked into the restaurant. Her silver blond hair fell soft and loose about her shoulders; the red wig was tucked safely away in her bag. Her jacket was reversed to the green and black plaid side, not going well with the smoke blue sunglasses perched on her nose.

A movement at a far table caught her eye. Having seen Lisa enter the restaurant, Slade was rising to meet her. Lisa's steps faltered as he moved toward her. She wasn't attempting to feign surprise at seeing him there. Her momentary uncertainty was caused by the panic racing through her veins. She managed to force it back and smile as they approached each other.

It wasn't really too difficult to smile warmly, not with his heart-disturbing look fanning the fires of her love. Slade halted, letting her cover the last few feet that would bring her to his side. Tall and darkly male, he stood before her, commanding all of her senses.

Unmindful of the other patrons in the restaurant, his dark head bent toward hers, stealing Lisa's breath in a hard kiss that was frustratingly brief for both of them. When he straightened, she swayed toward him and his arm curved around her shoulders to guide her toward the table.

"Hello." His low, belated greeting was husky and caressing. "You didn't expect to see me here, did you?"

"No, Mitzi didn't mention you would be joining us," Lisa could say truthfully.

The smoldering light in his eyes seemed to physically and lovingly touch each of her features, making her want to melt under the fiery glow. The possessive curve of his arm added to the boneless sensation.

"Sunday was the longest day of my life," Slade offered for her hearing alone.

"For me, too," Lisa admitted softly. They were nearly at the table where Mitzi waited, and Lisa had to tear her gaze from its adoring inspection of Slade's ruggedly handsome face. "Hello, Mitzi." But her voice still echoed the velvet quality induced by the magic of Slade's nearness. "I'm sorry I'm late."

"I didn't mind waiting, although I think Slade did." There was a knowing and pleased gleam in her aunt's eyes as she studied the two of them together.

Lisa flushed warmly as she sat in the chair Slade held out for her. Bending forward, Slade pushed her chair to the table, his face relatively close to her hair.

"Do you know something?" He took the chair to her left, a faintly bemused smile on his mouth. "You wear the same fragrance of perfume that my secretary does."

Lisa stiffened, every muscle tensing, every nerve alert to the danger of comparisons. "Really?" Her response was much too cool.

"Jealous?" he mocked laughingly, not seeming to care how much of their new relationship he was revealing to Mitzi. "You needn't be. It explains how you've seemed to haunt my every waking moment with the suggestion of you."

"It's a popular fragrance, sold at most cosmetic counters," she assured him.

"It suits Lisa well, though," Mitzi inserted. "Adult and evocative without being too cloyingly sweet."

"Speaking of suiting Lisa, I like your outfit," Slade complimented. "I would never have chosen green as your color, but you look beautiful in it."

"Thank you," Lisa responded nervously.

"Of course green is her color," her aunt spoke up. "Why shouldn't it be, with those—" The waiter appeared, opportunely for Lisa, with glasses and a chilled bottle of champagne.

"Champagne!" Lisa was delighted to interrupt Mitzi and keep her from remarking on the green of her eyes. "We really are going to celebrate the completion of your book!"

Minutes later the three of them were lifting their glasses as Slade toasted, "To your newest book. May it be the most successful one yet. Congratulations."

For a time the conversation was focused on Mitzi's new book, its plot and characters, and Lisa was able to relax. When Slade refilled the glasses, Lisa automatically reached for hers to take a sip of champagne, but Slade stopped her.

"Wait." His hand moved to the inside pocket of his suit jacket. "I don't mean to steal your thunder, Mitzi, but we have something else to celebrate."

Puzzled, Lisa didn't understand what he meant until she saw the velvet ring box in his hand. She breathed in softly when he snapped it open to reveal the rainbow brilliance of a diamond ring.

"I didn't intend to give this to you until tonight," he told her huskily, "but when I found out we'd be having lunch together, I couldn't wait. Give me your hand, Lisa."

She was too overcome with joy to speak or move. Happiness radiated from the shimmering tears in her eyes as she gazed at him. There was an equal depth of feeling in the glowing darkness of his own eyes. Smiling, Slade took hold of her left hand and drew it over to him. Immediately a deep frown was carved into his face.

"What is this?" he demanded.

Blinking in confusion, Lisa looked down at her hand, paling at the sight of the golden wedding band on her third finger. She had forgotten to switch rings. Quickly she tore it from her finger.

"It's a friendship ring the girls gave me this morning," she lied desperately. "It was too small to wear on my right hand."

She couldn't tell whether Slade believed her or not. The gold ring seemed to burn a circle in the tightly closed palm of her right hand, but she was afraid to put it in her bag for fear Slade would glimpse the red wig hidden inside.

"I'll take it to the jewelers for you and have it made larger," Slade offered, watching her closely.

"That isn't necessary," Lisa refused, and hurriedly slipped the gold band into her jacket pocket. "I can do it."

"Hurry and put the ring on her finger, Slade," Mitzi urged. "I want to see it."

Her hand was shaking badly as he slipped the diamond ring on her third finger. It never occurred to her to refuse it. When Slade smiled at her, all masculine and virile, Lisa knew that she loved him no matter what.

"Do you like it?" he asked.

"It's beautiful," she smiled.

"It's stunning, is the word!" Mitzi exclaimed, reaching for Lisa's hand to examine the ring more closely. "The two of you have made me the happiest woman in the world. I should have known something like this would happen when the two of you struck sparks off each other the instant you met."

"Didn't I tell you that's what she'd say?" Slade mocked.

"When is the wedding to be?" Mitzi wanted to know, still admiring the ring.

"Soon," Slade promised with typical self-assurance. "Very soon."

A toast was proposed by Mitzi, followed by more talk before they gave their luncheon order to the waiter. But all the while Lisa was plagued by stirrings of unease.

There was nothing in Slade's attitude to make her feel that way. She still received the touch of his hand and the warm caress of his gaze. The problem seemed to be solely her own—a guilty conscience.

After the meal was served and the dishes subsequently cleared, neither Mitzi nor Slade seemed inclined to bring the luncheon gathering to an end. Lisa was intensely conscious of the passing time, aware that the minute hand of her watch was inching near the one-thirty mark. And Ann Eldridge was supposed to have only an hour lunch break.

Twice she tried to make excuses to leave, but each time Slade used his persuasive charm to see that she didn't. Being newly engaged, Lisa could hardly reveal how eager—how anxious she was to leave, and she finally had to wait for one of them to make the first move.

Seconds ticked rapidly away before Slade glanced absently at his watch and sighed. "It's nearly two o'clock. As much as I hate to leave you, I have to get back to the office."

"I understand," Lisa assured him, smiling with relief.

Rising from his chair, he rested a hand on her shoulder, saying his goodbyes first to Mitzi before glancing down at Lisa. "I'll see you at seven tonight if not before."

"Yes," she agreed, lifting her head to receive the brushing kiss from his mouth.

There was no hope of beating him back to the office, not when she had to change into Ann Eldridge somewhere along the way. So she lingered for several more minutes with Mitzi before resorting to the much-used pretext of meeting Susan and Peg as the reason she couldn't return with Mitzi to her home.

"Run along," her aunt insisted, not raising a single objection to the news that she would again be denied Lisa's company. "I know how eager you must be to show off your engagement ring to your friends."

"Yes, I am," Lisa said, agreeing with the excuse and hurrying from the restaurant.

CHAPTER NINE

THIS TIME LISA did not overlook any minor details like rings when making her hasty change of identity. She was secure in that knowledge when she, Ann Eldridge, walked into the office. But that didn't stop her from quailing under the piercing look from Slade.

"Do you realize it's past two o'clock?" He stood beside her desk, tall and imposing.

"I'm sorry. I know I was late, but I didn't realize it was that time already." She apologized profusely, and began the speech she had been rehearsing since leaving the restaurant. "My dentist was running late in his appointments. Then, just as I got in the chair, an emergency came in—some little boy had his permanent front teeth knocked out and the doctor tried to save them. I shouldn't have waited, but they didn't think it would take very long. It turned out that it did and I'm late. If you want me to, I'll stay on later tonight to make up for it."

"There's no need for that." Slade appeared to relent slightly after hearing her explanation.

To reach her desk, Lisa had to walk around him. She did so reluctantly, depositing her handbag in a lower desk drawer before sitting in her chair and attempting to assume a professional posture.

"I'm glad you're so understanding about this." She smiled nervously. "When you gave me permission to leave early, I never intended to take advantage of you this way."

"I'm sure you didn't," he responded smoothly. "I came back only a few minutes ago myself."

Lisa felt the tension mounting to a screaming pitch. "Did you?" The brightness of her reply was forced. "It seems we both overextended our lunch hour."

"And both of us had cause. You, with your troubles at the dentist, and me," Slade paused, "I became engaged this noon."

"Really? Congratulations! That's wonderful news, Mr. Blackwell." She had never felt so small in all her life.

"Yes, it is." A complacent smile curved his mouth.

Having made this announcement, Lisa expected him to leave her, but he didn't. He continued to stand beside her desk. Her poise would splinter soon if he didn't go.

"Was there anything else, Mr. Blackwell?" She tried to prod him into leaving. "Will you be taking the rest of the afternoon off? Or did you want something?"

"There is one thing—" Slade paused.

"I'd like to buy my fiancée an engagement present. I wondered if you would have a suggestion."

"I have never met her so I really wouldn't know what to suggest." She could hear the breathless quality to her voice that revealed her inner agitation.

"What did your husband buy you for an engagement gift? Maybe that will help me," he said.

Lisa swallowed nervously. "He...he didn't have

enough money to buy me anything. He could barely afford the ring when we got engaged." She hated all these lies. They were tearing at her soul.

"You said your husband was in construction, didn't you?" Slade seemed to tower above the desk. Despite his seeming interest in the personal life of Ann Eldridge, Lisa felt increasingly uneasy.

"Yes, that's right," she murmured and began moving papers around on her desk to give her trembling hands something to do.

"What company does he work for? I'm familiar with a great many of them here in Charleston," he said.

Lisa wouldn't have been surprised if he knew every single one—which made it impossible for her to make up a fictitious company.

"I've forgotten what firm it is," she pleaded ignorance.

"You've forgotten." His gaze narrowed. "What would you do if there was an emergency and you had to get in touch with him? How can you explain forgetting the name of your husband's company?"

"I don't know." Lisa faked an indifferent shrug and struggled to bluff her way out of the corner. "If it's a dire emergency, I'll find a way to contact him."

"Is that how you explain it?"

"Yes." Her voice sounded small.

"Then I would like you to explain what this—" he reached down and opened her desk drawer, revealing Mitzi's file folder lying on top of the other papers "—is doing in your drawer."

"That folder?" Her throat was dry and her heart pumped wildly in fear. "It was among the stack of papers you gave me to be filed. I didn't get that one filed away before I left this noon, so I put it in my drawer rather than leave it lying out."

"I see." he murmured.

"I'll, er, file it now," Lisa stammered. Her hand was shaking as she picked up the folder and walked to the filing cabinets.

Slade followed leisurely to watch, his continued presence in the room scraping her nerves raw. She didn't know how much more she could stand.

"Did you have time to eat anything for lunch?" he asked unexpectedly as she went through the file drawer to find the proper place to put Mitzi's folder.

"No, I didn't," Lisa lied, "but that's all right. I should watch my weight anyway." She immediately regretted the allusion to her shape as his gaze skimmed her figure, setting off sensual shockwaves that vibrated her taut nerve ends.

"I've been meaning to compliment you on the outfit you're wearing. It's very attractive." Slade lightly traced the pointed collar of her jacket, his touch paralyzing her as if it was lethal. "It would be more striking in green, though, to match your eyes."

When he began to run his finger down the buttoned front of the jacket, Lisa regained control of her muscles and flinched from his touch.

"Please, Mr. Blackwell, don't do that." Her protest was breathy with alarm.

"'Don't do that, Mr. Blackwell!'" His angrily sarcastic mimicry of her protest startled Lisa.

The words were still ringing in her ears when her arm was caught and she was yanked roughly against him. The breath was knocked from her lungs by the unyielding contact with his muscular chest.

She never had a chance to regain it as her lips were crushed against her teeth by the brutal assault of his mouth. For unending moments Slade plundered the softness of her lips, savagely ravishing them until she had not the strength to resist if she had found the will.

When he was finished wreaking his anger on her, he let her go. Lisa reeled backward, her hands seeking the support of the sturdy metal cabinets. But Slade wasn't quite through with her. He followed her, arms stretched against the cabinet on either side of her, trapping her there to face his proud fury.

"What kind of a fool do you think I am?" he snarled.

"Slade, let me explain." Her heart was hammering in her throat and she could hardly breathe. Her legs were still shaking from the raging anger in his kiss.

"Just because I didn't see through your charade in the beginning, did you think I'd go right on being blind, Lisa?" A muscle twitched convulsively in his jaw, indicating how very tenuous his hold was on his temper.

"You don't understand," she protested.

"I understand very well. When I saw that wedding band on your finger today, all the pieces began to fall into place." His voice was flat and hard, riddled with contempt and disgust.

If Lisa had been given a moment of warning, some little sign that she was about to be unmasked, she might have been better able to defend herself. But no, Slade had let her tell more lies, given indications that he believed them, then pounced like a sleek panther on an unwary prey. She was completely at his mercy—or his lack of it.

"I—" she began, intimidated by his sheer masculinity and the ruthless set of his hard jaw.

"No more lies, Lisa!" Slade slashed away her attempt to explain, looming closer to her as if he would silence her forever.

Lisa flattened herself against the filing cabinet, the metal cool to the hands she spread against its surface. Her left arm was seized and twisted upward by steel fingers.

"Where is my ring?" he accused.

The pain he was causing her was more than just physical. There was the mental anguish of his slicing voice, wounding her heart with its ability to hurt deeply. When she didn't answer immediately, he increased the pressure on her arm, unaware of how fierce his grip was.

"In my pocket," she answered, biting back the cry of pain.

"It never had a chance to be warmed by your skin before you were slipping it off," Slade muttered savagely. Swiftly he made the change to sarcasm, lifting her left hand to force the gold wedding band into her view. "You slipped it off to put on this." His upper lip curled in a sneer.

"Give me a chance—"

"No!" The denial seemed to explode from him as his free hand fastened itself around her throat. His glittering look was darkly menacing, intensified by the coldly ruthless line of his mouth. "You've had your last chance."

But Lisa wasn't really frightened. She seemed to know instinctively that no matter how great his anger was toward her, Slade would never harm her physically. He didn't need to, not when he could cut her heart into ribbons with words.

The door to the reception area opened and Drew came sauntering into Lisa's office. He came to an abrupt halt at the sight of them, his mouth opening for a speechless second.

"Slade, what the hell are you doing?" He demanded in a voice that sounded positive he was seeing things. A disbelieving frown creased his forehead. "Ann—"

"No, not Ann." Slade's hand left her throat to grab a handful of the red wig.

Gasping in pain, Lisa caught at his wrist to stop him. "Slade, it's pinned!"

"Then unpin it and take the damned thing off!" He released her completely and took a step away, anger vibrating from him even as he remained motionless.

While Lisa shakily removed the hairpins that secured the wig to her scalp, no one uttered a word. Drew was stunned and confused, especially when silver blond hair tumbled to Lisa's shoulders. There wasn't any satisfaction in Slade's angrily grim expression at the completion of the task. He took the wig from her unresisting fingers.

"Here." He turned to Drew and tossed him the scarlet-haired wig. "You always claimed to be partial to redheads. Take it and get out!"

In reflex action, Drew had caught it. Now he stared at it, not quite able to take in what was going on. "But—" He looked back at Slade and frowned.

"Out!" was the acid command.

Glancing uncertainly at Lisa, Drew finally turned and hesitantly retreated to the reception area, closing the door quietly behind him. Slade's attention returned to her, but Lisa sensed that Drew's interruption had given him a measure of control he hadn't previously had.

He stared at her, assessing her with narrowed eyes. "The wig was an excellent red herring, Lisa, if you'll pardon the expression," he jeered. "I never suspected for an instant that Ann and Lisa were the same person, but that's what you counted on, wasn't it?"

"Yes." It was foolish to deny it. Lisa lifted a weary hand to brush the hair from her face, letting it stay at the back of her neck and pressing her fingers against the throbbing tenseness that was there.

"And your lying green eyes," he snapped. "Equaled only by the falsehoods that come so easily from your lips."

For the second time she was hauled roughly against him. Her heart fluttered a warning before his mouth closed over hers to kiss her long and hungrily—and angrily. Her lips were parted by the bruising urgency of his. For a few delirious moments, she thrilled to the passion of his love, deepening the kiss with a fiery response of her own.

His arms circled her to hold her in their vice, while her own hands spread over his muscled shoulders. Just when she thought Slade loved her enough to forgive her for deceiving him, he broke off the kiss. Her eyes fluttered open to see the self-disgust and contempt that thinned his mouth. The pain to her heart was swift and stabbing.

A moan of protest came from her throat as she rested her forehead against him. "No matter what else you think about me, you must know that I love you, Slade."

Violently she was thrust from him, long impatient strides cleaving a distance between them. Several feet away he stopped, muscles rigid, to glare over his shoulder.

"Do you really love me?" Slade taunted cynically. "Or is it simply convenient to love me?"

"No," Lisa denied in a choked voice. "It isn't convenient to love you."

Not when she was faced with the dilemma of either keeping silent about his unethical if not illegal use of Mitzi's money or exposing him. If she didn't love him, the choice would be much easier to make. In fact, there probably wouldn't even be the need for a choice.

Slade turned his head away, tipping it back to stare at the ceiling. "It's amazing how I could have been so blind not to see it before now," he sighed bitterly, lowering his head with a grim shake. "Everything clicks into place now like the pieces of a puzzle, fitting perfectly. No wonder you didn't have any secretarial skills. You aren't a secretary. The agency people have never heard of you, have they?"

"No," Lisa admitted.

"And I opened the door for you when I mistook you for one of their girls," he muttered with a sharp edge of irony. "There's nothing wrong with your eyes, either. You only wore those sunglasses to hide their color, didn't you?"

"Yes, there's nothing wrong with—" .

"And your two girl friends, you invented them to

explain your whereabouts during the day to Mitzi so she wouldn't wonder where you were spending your time. You don't have any old college friends in Charleston, do you?" Slade accused.

"None that I know—"

"Which explains why you were so unfamiliar with the sights of the city," he interrupted coldly. "You haven't seen anything, not even Brookgreen Gardens. That's why you didn't remember the basket stands along the highway. Because you'd never been anywhere close to them."

"Okay, so I haven't," Lisa retorted in a frustrated spurt of defiance.

His needle-sharp words were painful. She couldn't continue to endure being the whipping boy for his anger. It wasn't in her nature to keep getting hurt without trying to hurt back.

Pivoting, Slade faced her, his hands on his hips in proud challenge, his dark gaze relentless searching her face. "The day I found you in my office supposedly straightening my papers, you were really going through them, weren't you? What were you looking for? The Talmadge folder?"

"Yes." Lisa tossed back her head, blinking at the tears that burned her eyes, refusing to shed one of them.

"Why? What did you hope to gain?" he demanded.

"I wanted to find out what you were doing with Mitzi's money," she answered truthfully and without apology.

"My God!" Slade muttered, cursing savagely beneath his breath.

"What did you expect me to do?" Lisa stormed. "Let you steal every dime of it?"

The tears nearly escaped to form a waterfall down her lashes. She barely managed to check their descent in time, glancing quickly away from him to open her green eyes as wide as she could and swallow the lump in her throat.

"And what did you find out when you got your greedy hands on the folder?" He was snarling, his teeth bared in challenge.

"Nothing!" she breathed in a rush. "I never had a chance to do more than open it!"

"And that's the way it's going to stay!" Slade declared. "Because you're through. Your charade is over and I don't want Lisa Talmadge in this office!"

Lisa gulped in a deep breath, held it for an instant and expelled it in a long, shuddering sigh. She couldn't meet the steel black quality of his eyes and glanced away. She should have known it would end like this.

"Do you know what's the matter with you, Slade Blackwell?" It was a taut challenge, flung out in the despair of heartbreak.

"Yes," he replied grimly. "I foolishly thought I could expect trust from someone like you."

Trust! Someone like you! The accusation hurt unbearably, because it came from Slade and because he didn't have the right to cast the first stone.

She was caught in the grip of an impotent kind of anger. Too many conflicting emotions had become trapped inside and had to be released. It was a jumbled assortment that came out, half love and half hate, a coin whose two sides had joined to make one.

"That isn't what's eating you," she denied with a

vigorous shake of her head. "No, it's your precious male ego. You can't stand it that I managed to fool you even for a few days. It's too damaging to your fragile male pride to be taken in by a mere inferior female. All you can think about is that I made a fool of you!"

He took a threatening step toward her, then checked himself. His glittering eyes scanned her pale features. Slade seemed to control his temper with difficulty.

"What are you trying to prove, Lisa?" he breathed raggedly. "That you can get under my skin without any effort?"

"No," Lisa answered tightly. "I just want you to admit what's really bothering you."

"You want to know what's really bothering me?" His jaw hardened into bronze. "I'm trying to figure out how I got myself engaged to a greedy little bitch like you."

Lisa recoiled as if he had slapped her face, the blood draining from her cheeks and her stomach muscles tying themselves in a nauseous lump. Shaking fingers searched frantically through the pockets of her jacket until they found the hard gemstone of his ring.

"That's easily remedied." Her voice was hoarse, the wounded cry of an animal in intense pain. "You can take your ring back and you won't have to wonder any more!"

In that fleeting moment when she had taken her attention from him, Slade had crossed the space that separated them. The diamond ring was stripped from her trembling hand and her left was captured.

"I am not taking it back!" he snapped, and began twisting the plain gold band from her third finger. Lisa struggled to free her left hand from his bruising grasp, but he was too strong for her. When the finger was bare, he roughly pushed on the diamond. "This ring is going on and it's staying on."

"No."

"Dammit, yes!" He gave her a hard shake that rattled her teeth. "When you leave here, you're going to march yourself straight to Mitzi's house and pretend that nothing has happened. Because nothing has. Nothing has changed."

"Hasn't it?" Lisa retorted bitterly.

"No, it hasn't," Slade informed her in a steely voice. "And when I get there tonight, you're going to pretend to be the happy bride-to-be that Mitzi expects to see."

"Why?" she breathed in protest.

"Because we're going to be married and you damned well better get used to the idea," he declared. "The only thing that's different now is I've found out about your lies. I don't know—maybe you're incapable of the truth. But you are going to be my wife, make no mistake about that."

"What—" Lisa hesitated, daring to hope "—about Mitzi's money?"

"You don't need to worry about that," he jeered. "Once we're married, what's mine is yours and what's yours is mine."

Lisa flinched, hurt. "Is that why you're marrying me?"

"Don't put that question in my mind," Slade ordered crisply. "Or I'll start asking myself if that's why you're marrying me."

"Slade—" she began earnestly.

"No!" He released her, breathing in deeply as he moved away. "No more talking, not until I've had a chance to think a few more things out. Go on back to Mitzi's." His mouth quirked cynically. "I'm sure you can come up with some story to explain why you're returning sooner than you planned."

"That was unnecessary," Lisa stiffened in resentment.

"I'll see you at six," Slade said, ignoring her comment with autocratic ease. "You be there."

"I will," she answered as curtly as he had given the order. "You have my word on that."

"I don't want your word," he snapped. "I just want you there."

Lisa stared at him silently through a mist of proud tears, then walked to the desk to retrieve her bag from the drawer. She could feel his gaze watching her every move, but he offered not one word of parting when she walked out of the door into the reception room.

Drew was sitting on the edge of the receptionist's desk when Lisa emerged. His searching look was echoed by the receptionist, curiosity gleaming on both their faces.

Lisa guessed that they were bound to have overheard some of what she and Slade had said. Neither of them had given much thought to the volume of their voices at times. Her gaze bounced away from them as she started toward the street door. Drew straightened from the desk.

"Ann—" he began uncertainly.

Lisa turned, meeting his questioning gaze directly. "The name is Lisa Talmadge."

"Talmadge?" he echoed in disbelief, but Lisa was already walking out the door onto the street.

CHAPTER TEN

LISA TWISTED HER HANDS nervously and stopped pacing as Mitzi entered the comfortably furnished living room. She had come to a decision, a difficult one that was already beginning to give her cold feet.

"Sl—" Her voice broke shrilly and she started again. "Slade will be here at six, Mitzi."

"Yes, you mentioned that before," her aunt replied with amused patience.

"Yes, I know," Lisa nodded, looking away in agitation. "If you don't mind, I'd like to speak to him alone for a few minutes."

"Well, of course you can," was the laughing response. "I'm not so old that I don't remember what it's like to be in love and wanting to be alone with the person you love."

"I don't mean it that way exactly," Lisa faltered, and breathed in deeply to try to control the clamoring of her nerves. "I want to be alone with Slade, but I want you to be in the next room."

"The next room?" Mitzi was plainly astonished by the request. "Whatever for? You surely don't think you're going to have to call me for help?"

"No, I—I want you there to listen." Lisa's gaze ricocheted from her aunt to the intertwining of her fingers.

"To listen?" Mitzi was even more astonished. "Why?"

"I don't know how to say this exactly, Mitzi, but—" She paused in agitation, ripping her fingers apart to run a hand over the side of her forehead into the pale blonde of her hair.

"Just say it," her aunt urged.

"I'm afraid Slade is—stealing from you." The accusation clawed its way out of her throat.

"What?" Mitzi's mouth remained open for several seconds before she frowned. "Is this some kind of a joke?" she breathed in a short laugh.

"I wish it were," Lisa declared in torment, "but it isn't."

"Whatever gave you this ridiculous idea?" was the frowning demand.

"I suspected he might be when I first came here. When I confronted him with my suspicions, he admitted it." Tears filled her eyes and Lisa had to turn to the window, blinking furiously to keep them at bay while she swallowed to ease the burning tightness in her throat.

"I don't believe you," Mitzi returned slowly, emphasizing the negative contraction.

"I didn't think you would." Lisa glanced sadly over her shoulder, gazing at her aunt with troubled green eyes. "That's why I tried to get proof."

"Proof?"

Lisa rushed on, not wanting to explain about Ann Eldridge and the lies she had been telling since her arrival. "I don't blame you for not believing me. That's why I want you to listen at the door. I'll...I'll get Slade to admit it again."

"Lisa." Mitzi walked to her niece, lightly taking Lisa by the shoulders and intently searching her face. "You really believe this, don't you?"

"Yes." It was a stiff little sound, teeth clenched to keep the pain in her chest from escaping in a sob.

"But at noon—you took his ring? You said you'd marry him?" Her aunt frowned.

"I'm afraid I really do love him, Mitzi." Lisa tried to smile, her chin quivering uncontrollably. "Isn't that the pits?" She tried to laugh at her foolishness, but it came out in an anguished sound.

"I'm sure there's some mistake," Mitzi insisted. "Slade—"

The doorbell rang and Lisa stiffened. "He's here." She looked frantically at her aunt. "Will you listen?"

Mitzi pursed her lips thoughtfully, then nodded a reluctant agreement. "But you've made some kind of mistake about Slade, Lisa, I'm sure of it."

"I wish you were right," Lisa sighed brokenly.

With a comforting squeeze of her shoulders, Mitzi let her go. "I'll answer the door and send Slade in here. I'll be outside."

Cowardlike, Lisa wanted to call the whole thing off as her aunt walked from the living room to the front door. But she was doing it for Slade as well as Mitzi. Breathing in deeply, she wiped the moistness from her lashes and faced the door when Slade entered the room.

He paused a few feet inside the living room to stare at her, a black shuttered look to his dark gaze. His saturnine features were carved in an aloof mask, hard and withdrawn. Yet Lisa's pulse leaped at the sight of him, tall and vital. Nothing could diminish that aura of virility that surrounded him, magnetically attracting her to his presence.

"I see you're here," Slade observed curtly.

"I told you I would be," she reminded him defensively.

"Yes—" he exhaled a cynical breath of amusement "—but your lying tongue has told me many things these past few days." Lisa flinched at the cutting gibe and he turned away, muttering, "I need a drink."

Long, impatient strides carried him to the drink trolley. He paused as he added ice cubes to a glass to let his dark gaze rake Lisa's rigidly erect form.

"You look as if you could use a drink, too," Slade noted in uncomplimentary fashion.

"No," she refused.

But Slade began pouring her one anyway. Her green eyes skittered a look to the door where she knew Mitzi was listening. Breathing in shakily to find courage, she walked stiffly to the drinks' cart.

"Slade, we have to talk," she said nervously.

"Here." He thrust a glass toward her, ice clinking against the sides.

"I don't want it," Lisa refused again.

"Take it," he snapped. His temper hadn't improved. It was only more tightly leashed.

Reluctantly she accepted it rather than let herself be sidetracked by an unimportant argument. The cold sides of the glass seemed to echo the chilling temperature that numbed her heart.

"We have to talk, Slade," she repeated.

"Yes," he agreed grimly, and took a long drink from

his glass. "Bob Turner is back." His gaze sliced to her. "I know you haven't met him, but I'm sure Drew told you about him. He's the third member of my legal team. I've arranged the schedule so that we can leave tomorrow for Baltimore. That will give me a chance to meet your parents before we're married."

"Slade—" Lisa tried to interrupt. That wasn't what she wanted to talk about at all.

"I'd like a private ceremony," he continued without so much as a glance to acknowledge her attempt, "with just the immediate family present. I imagine you would prefer to have it conducted in Baltimore where your family is. I can't see any reason why it can't be arranged to take place within a week."

"Stop it!" Tears welled in her eyes, the shimmering pools intensifying the olive green darkness of her pupils.

"I'll stop nothing!" The shuttered look lifted briefly to reveal the anger that still blazed within. "We will be married, Lisa."

"That isn't what I want to talk about," she protested. "There are other things."

"Such as?" Slade taunted.

The shutters were closed again. The tears threatening to flow from her eyes had been noticed, but they didn't soften his hard features.

"Such as Mitzi," Lisa choked.

"What about Mitzi?" He swirled the liquor in his glass, watching the spinning ice cubes. "She'll be invited to the wedding, of course."

"You know that's not what I want to talk about," she hurled in a tormented whisper.

"No, it's never what you want to talk about when you mention Mitzi, is it?" Slade taunted acidly. "It's always her money. I told you this afternoon not to worry about it any more. Once we're married it'll take care of itself. I'll handle it from now on."

"How much—" It was difficult to get the words out. "How much have you taken from Mitzi already?"

"What's the matter, Lisa?" His lip curled sarcastically as he lifted the glass to his mouth. "Are you afraid I'll cheat you out of your share?"

Lisa paled but refused to let him avoid the question. "How much?"

Downing the rest of his drink, Slade glared at the empty glass. "Is the money that damned important to you?"

"Isn't it to you?" she countered.

"Dammit, Lisa!" The glass was slammed onto the trolley, bottles rattling loudly at the suppressed violence in his action. "I—"

"I'm sorry, Lisa." Mitzi's voice came from the doorway, bubbling with inner laughter. "I couldn't stand out in the hallway another minute." Lisa turned with a jerk, staring at her aunt in dismay. "I can't make up my mind if I was listening to a tragic comedy or a comic tragedy!"

Slade turned on Lisa, towering above her in an icy rage. "You arranged for Mitzi to be outside listening?" he accused savagely.

"Yes," she admitted weakly.

"Lisa came to me this afternoon with this nonsense about you stealing from me," Mitzi explained, with an indulging smile at her niece. "I tried to convince her how ridiculous the idea was, but she simply wouldn't listen to me. So I agreed to listen outside. I never heard such silliness in all my life!"

"I was trying to do what I thought was best," Lisa defended tightly.

"Best for whom?" Slade challenged, his mouth thinning whitely in anger. Abruptly, he turned away. "Never mind, don't answer that. I can guess."

"Lisa is certain she's doing it for your own good." High amusement laced Mitzi's voice. "I don't know what game you're playing, Slade, but I think you should put the poor girl straight. It's tearing her apart."

"I'll bet," he jeered, rubbing an angry hand across the back of his neck.

The telephone rang and the housekeeper's shuffling footsteps could be heard in the hall as she went to answer it. Lisa gazed achingly at Slade's taut figure. She knew that he thought she had exposed him simply to get into Mitzi's sole favor. And it hurt.

"It's for you, Mitzi," the housekeeper called with sighing patience.

Her aunt glanced briefly at Lisa, giving her an encouraging smile that said everything would be all right. Lisa wished she could believe Mitzi as her aunt left the room.

At the closing of the door, Slade sighed, "I can't believe you actually did this, Lisa."

"What else could I do?" she cried in frustration. "I couldn't let you go on stealing from her!"

"No, you couldn't do that!" he hurled sarcastically. "There might not be anything left for you!"

"What does it matter, Slade?" Lisa protested. "She doesn't believe me."

"Thank heaven," he muttered.

"Even if she did, she'd forgive you. I don't know how much you've taken, Slade, but give it back. Mitzi loves you almost as much as I do. She wouldn't turn you in, not if you paid back all the money you've taken."

"What?" Slade turned, frowning as he stared into Lisa's entreating green eyes.

"I can help. I can find a job here in Charleston and earn—" She didn't have a chance to complete her offer as Slade fluidly crossed the space to capture her shoulders.

"What are you saying?" he demanded, eyeing her warily. "I thought you were after Mitzi's money."

"No, I only pretended—"

"You mean you lied about that, too!" His frown was starting to change into a disbelieving smile.

"You have to understand, Slade," Lisa tried to explain. His touch was playing havoc with her senses, making it difficult to think straight. "I was trying to protect Mitzi." She stared at his shirt collar, aware of his dark gaze inspecting her face. "I let you think I was after her money, too, hoping you would make a slip and give me proof that you were stealing from her. I knew Mitzi wouldn't believe me without proof because she cares about you too much. It never occurred to me that I might begin to care for you." His shoulders were shaking. Lisa couldn't look up, afraid to see tears staining his proud face. "Let alone fall in love with you. Give the money back, Slade. We don't need it."

A low rolling sound started. Lisa flinched, closing

her eyes at what she thought was a groan of suffering and hopefully remorse. Then it exploded into chuckling laughter, deep and throaty and riddled with amusement. In disbelief, she looked up to see Slade's head thrown back, a smile splitting his male lips.

"I don't see anything funny about that!" she breathed with a trace of temper.

"Don't you?" The glittering warmth of his gaze inspected her indignant expression, laughing and bright. "Oh, Lisa—" he sighed in what sounded very much like contentment "—I haven't taken a cent of Mitzi's money."

"Thank goodness!" she shuddered in relief.

"What's more—" he curved a finger under her chin and tipped her head up "—I never had any intention of taking her money."

"But—" Lisa frowned with bewilderment "—you said—"

"I never said I had," Slade reminded her gently. "I let you believe it because you were already so convinced that it was true."

"But you wanted us to join forces!" Lisa stared at him, wanting desperately to believe what he said, but unable to ignore the lingering doubts.

"Because I thought you were after Mitzi's money. I've become very fond of your aunt these past few years. She seems like my own. I was trying to protect her from you. And all the while, you were trying to protect her from me."

"Oh." It was a tiny sound that slowly curved her mouth into a smile. "Oh, Slade!" She began to laugh, too, at the sheer ridiculousness of the whole thing.

His arms circled around her, holding her close as he joined in her laughter. The warmth of his body heat melted the chill that had encased her heart. Lisa felt alive again, deliriously alive and happy.

"What a pair of liars we are!" Slade chuckled against her hair.

Lisa raised her head, leaning against him. "But I've never lied about my feelings," she told him, lost in the enchantment of his spell. "I never lied about loving you, Slade."

"And I never lied about loving you," he said as he lowered his mouth to hers.